Harper

A Road to Romance Mystery

By

Kathi Daley

This book is a work of fiction. Names, characters, places, and incidents either are products of the author's imagination or are used fictitiously. Any resemblance to actual events or locales or persons, living or dead, is entirely coincidental.

Copyright © 2023 by Katherine Daley

Version 2.0

Chapter 1

Harper Hathaway glanced at the San Francisco skyline as it faded into the distance with the conviction that of all the Hathaway sisters, she was going to go down in family history as having made the biggest mess of her life. Not that making a mess of her life had been what she'd set out to do fourteen years ago, when she'd fled her hometown of Moosehead, Minnesota, feeling lost and alone in a sea of family and friends. She'd recently graduated high school and had been expected to come up with a plan as to what to do with her life, which at the time seemed pretty overwhelming. Despite a family who loved her, a boyfriend who wanted to marry her, and a grade point average that would have landed her a spot in almost any college in the country, she'd had absolutely no idea who or what she wanted to be. So, after weeks of sleepless nights and angst-filled days, she'd hitched her wagon to the first opportunity she stumbled upon and joined the Army after a recruiter made a cold call to a young woman who actually *was* looking for a life of meaningful adventure in addition to a career.

Looking back, things had worked out all right. At least for a time. Yes, she'd missed her family, and those first years overseas were some of the hardest she'd ever known, but she seemed to have a skill set and personality type that fit well with the lifestyle presented to her, and she'd risen through the ranks at a speed that at times had left her downright dizzy. When time came to re-up after her first tour, she hadn't even considered other options and happily signed on the dotted line. By the time her second contract was complete she was on the fast track to a career with Special Forces, but by the time she'd completed her third contract, she'd seen enough death and destruction to last her a lifetime. She knew in her heart she was ready to try something different and had considered going home to Moosehead, but then she met Eric Palmer, a scuba-diving instructor with a taste for treasure hunting, a bit of wanderlust, and big dreams for the future. Deciding to follow the man and his passion, she moved to San Diego, became a certified scuba diver herself, and followed Eric from one exotic locale to the next. Not only had they traveled the world in search of the ultimate dive site, but they'd joined salvage operations along the way. For a brief period in time, she'd really had it all: an exciting life that challenged her both physically and intellectually, a fiancé on the same life path that she had grown to love, and a bright future limited only by what she could imagine. Then, six months ago, her perfect world came tumbling down when her fiancé was killed while diving on a wreck in Cozumel and she'd lost her will to continue down the path they'd chosen to walk together. So, one hundred and sixty-nine months, two weeks, and eight days after she'd left her home in pursuit of a new life, she found herself returning to Minnesota the same lost and lonely mess she was on the day she'd left.

As she veered from the freeway onto the narrow coastal highway that would take her north, she felt her mood lighten. As a teen, she'd felt stifled in such a small town, but now that her life was such a mess, she realized that after fourteen years out in the world, a large farm perched on a private lake seemed like the optimal place to regroup and heal. As she navigated the narrow, winding road that hugged the rocky shoreline, she tried not to think about what she'd lost. She knew in her heart if she was going to ever be able to move forward, she had to find a way to stop looking back at what might have been.

After she had driven for several hours, the open coastline gave way to the dense forest of the redwoods. Without the crashing waves to set the mood, her mind began to wander and the fatigue she had been holding at bay began to creep into her consciousness. Deciding that what she really needed was a diversion, she reached forward to switch on the radio. She was momentarily distracted as she searched for a station, which was probably why she hadn't seen the dog that darted onto the road until a split second before it ran in front of her. She slammed on her brakes and turned the wheel hard to the left. She somehow managed to guide the vehicle to a stop, but not before she lost control of it and slid into a drainage ditch that bordered the road. Her heart was pounding a mile a minute by the time she came to a full stop.

She put her hand over her chest. She wasn't hurt, and while the car was going to need to be towed, she didn't think it was badly damaged. She put her hand on the latch and opened the driver's side door. Taking a deep breath to steady shaky knees, she slowly climbed out. She was pretty sure she was fine, but the dog… She looked around the area and didn't see a dog, injured or otherwise. She didn't think she'd hit him. She slowly made her way up the embankment and looked around. She couldn't see the dog, but after a moment she heard him whimpering from the other side of the road. The sun had set and the sky was beginning to grow dim, so she pulled on her jacket, grabbed the flashlight she kept for emergencies, and jogged across the road. "Are you okay?"

The yellow Labrador, which was really no more than a puppy, continued to whine, so she walked slowly forward. "I won't hurt you," she said in a soft voice. "I just want to help." The pup didn't move, and he didn't attack either, so she took a few more steps. Not only had she grown up on a farm but her mother was a veterinarian. She'd lived around animals her entire life and generally knew how to calm them. She could see that this one was scared, but he also seemed to want her to help.

"I'm going to come closer," she said in a soft voice.

The dog watched her warily but didn't move toward her. When she was within a few feet of him, he moved away. She took a few more steps. He moved a few of his own. She supposed at some point he must have realized that she was going to continue to follow because he limped down the embankment and into the dense forest. He hadn't gone far when she noticed something blue. A car. The dog had led her to a car that must have veered off the road. There was still steam coming from its engine compartment, so she had to assume the accident had recently occurred.

She made her way toward the car as fast as the steep terrain would allow, slipping only once on the muddy ground. When she reached the car, she headed directly to the open driver's side door and looked inside. There was a man in the seat who was still buckled in with a large gash on his head. He appeared to be unconscious. She looked into the interior of the vehicle and found a woman in the passenger seat. She likewise appeared to be unconscious. Taking a quick peek into the rear of the vehicle, she saw a baby strapped into a car seat.

"A baby," she said a little too loudly. She must have startled the dog because he began to bark aggressively. "It's okay," she said in a gentler voice. "I'm going to go around to the back and open the door so I can see what needs to be done. Okay?"

The dog stopped barking but didn't move from the position he had taken up near the open driver's side door. When she arrived at the back door, Harper assured the dog once again that he could trust her. She opened the door and gently ran her hands over the baby, who was awake and appeared to be unharmed. She unstrapped the car seat, lifted the baby out, and cradled the whimpering infant in her arms. "It's okay. I have you now. It's okay. I'm going to get help."

She walked back around to the front of the vehicle to check on the driver. She felt for a pulse, and he opened his eyes. "The baby," he gasped. "You need to hide the baby."

"Hide the baby?"

"Hurry. You must leave now. Don't trust anyone."

She froze in indecision. The man had lost a lot of blood. She had to wonder if he was delirious. She looked toward the woman in the passenger seat and realized for the first time that she had a gunshot wound in her chest. "The baby's mother?"

The man nodded. "Dead. Now hurry. Take the diaper bag. It is up to you to keep the baby safe."

She looked down at the infant in her arms. He or she appeared to have drifted off. She didn't feel right about leaving the man and woman in the car and was trying to make up her mind about the options available to her when she heard another car on the road. She wasn't sure why she made the decision to hide. Instinct, she supposed. One minute she was contemplating the idea of calling 911 and the next she was heading toward the cover of the trees with the baby cradled snuggly in her arms and the long strap of the diaper bag draped over her shoulder. The puppy, who seemed to have settled down now that she had the baby, trailed along behind her.

After a few minutes of searching for an adequate hiding place, she found an outcropping of rocks that, combined with the darkening sky, seemed to provide sufficient cover. She tightened one arm around the baby, caressed the puppy with the other, crouched down as low as she could manage, and watched as a man in a highway patrol uniform hiked down the embankment, walked over to the car, said something to the driver, took out a gun, and shot him. The pup began to growl. She shushed him and then watched as the patrolman walked around the vehicle and shot the woman in the passenger seat, although, according to the driver of the vehicle, she was already dead. The accident hadn't appeared to have been serious enough to be responsible for the woman's death, so Harper had to assume she had died from the bullet wound to her chest. After he shot the woman in the passenger seat, the officer opened the back door and stuck his head inside. She held her breath when she realized that he must be looking for the baby. After rooting around in the rear of the vehicle for a moment, he took several steps away from it and looked around.

Her heart pounded as she continued to crouch behind the rocks, calming the puppy and whispering to the baby. It was a cold day in Early December and the blanket in which someone had wrapped the baby wasn't all that heavy, so Harper unzipped her jacket, slipped the baby inside, and then scrunched down even smaller and waited. The puppy climbed into her lap, providing an extra layer of warmth for the baby as the man in the uniform continued to search the immediate area. The tall, thin man, with dark hair and a crooked nose, took several steps in her direction, pausing only a few yards from the rocks where she was hiding. If not for her military training, she was certain she would have screamed or fainted or both. The baby let out a tiny cry, so she tightened her arms around the bundle she'd nestled to her chest and prayed the puppy would remain quiet and the baby would go back to sleep.

After a few minutes, the man headed back toward the vehicle for a second look, opened both the trunk and the engine compartment, rooted around, circled back toward them, and then pulled out his phone and spoke in a deep voice. "Agent Beaverton is dead, as is the witness. The baby is gone and there is no sign of the ledger. There is a car in the ditch just off the road. I assume that its driver found our target and went for help. I'm going to see if there's ID inside the vehicle. The driver can't have gotten far."

Harper watched as the man turned and headed back toward the road. After he'd driven away, she scooted out from behind the rocks and let out a long breath of relief before the puppy, the baby, and she slowly made their way back toward her car. It was almost completely dark now and getting colder by the minute. She knew she needed to get help, but her car was disabled, and a quick search of her vehicle confirmed that the man who had shot the occupants of the vehicle carrying the baby had taken her purse and her phone, as well as her vehicle registration.

"Okay, this can't be good," she mumbled. She supposed it made sense to stay with the vehicle. Someone would come along eventually. Of course, the man who had been with the baby had said not to trust anyone, and it had been a man in a highway patrolman's uniform who had shot and killed him in cold blood. Maybe waiting with the car wasn't the best idea. She'd been heading toward a small town she knew was just north of her position when the accident occurred. The town was still quite a way off, but she'd driven this road before, and she seemed to remember a rundown little motel connected to a gas station and a small eatery not all that far up the road. Staying in a motel so close to the spot where her car had been disabled might not be the smartest thing to do given the fact that there was at least one man she knew of looking for the baby she'd tucked beneath her jacket. Still, staying with the car was probably the worst thing she could do, so she began to walk along the side of the road with the baby in her arms and the puppy trailing along beside her. The baby hadn't been very active since she'd plucked it from its car seat. This, she had to admit, worried her. Had it been hurt in the accident despite the lack of blood? He or she had been strapped into a high-quality infant car carrier that appeared to have shielded the tiny thing from the worst of the impact, but she supposed the infant could have sustained internal injuries. She didn't have a lot of options at this point, so she hiked the diaper bag more firmly over her shoulder and continued to walk, praying all the while that a solution to her dilemma would present itself before it was too late.

******

"'Closed for the season.'" She groaned as she read the sign nailed to the front of the motel, gas station, and eatery she'd remembered. It had taken her forty minutes of steady walking to arrive here, and she couldn't remember there being another town for a good twenty to thirty miles more. She needed to get the baby inside and out of the cold, so, making a quick decision, she made her way over to the small motel and used the multiuse knife she always kept in her pocket to break into one of the rooms farthest away from the road. Once the puppy, the baby, and she were inside, she tried the lights, but the electricity was turned off. She used the flashlight she still had in her pocket to provide at least a modicum of light. She unzipped her jacket, removed the bundled-up baby, and laid it on the bed. The puppy jumped up onto the bed and stretched out next to it.

"Hey, sweetie, how are you doing?" she cooed to the child.

The baby opened its eyes.

"I know that you are probably wet and hungry. Hopefully, there will be supplies in the bag that will take care of both those problems."

She slid the diaper bag off her shoulder and emptied its contents onto the bed. A package of diapers, baby wipes, a can of powdered formula, several bottles of purified water, a couple of pairs of warm pajamas, and a thumb drive. Everything made sense except the thumb drive. She slipped the drive into her pocket and unwrapped the baby from the blanket. She took off the wet diaper to find that her traveling companion was a little girl. She quickly changed the baby's diaper, then dressed her in the warmest pajamas she could find. Once she was clean and dry, she wrapped her in the blanket she'd found her in, then pulled the blanket from the bed over her as well. Harper had no way of knowing when the baby had last been fed, but her tiny little whimper seemed like a *feed me* sort of cry, so she read the instructions on the can of formula, mixed up a bottle, and then held it to the baby's lips. She took a single suck, then began to cry. The bottle was ice cold, and having had three younger sisters, Harper could remember that babies liked to have their bottles warmed. She made sure the baby was tucked securely on the bed, then went into the bathroom, praying for hot water. Just because the electricity was off didn't mean the gas was off as well.

She held her breath as she turned on the faucet. The water was ice cold at first, but after a moment it began to warm up. She filled the basin with hot water, then held the bottle in it until the formula felt warmer. She made her way back to the bed, arranged the pillows against the headboard, and leaned into them as she cradled the baby in her arms. Thankfully, she devoured the bottle as the puppy snuggled in next to them and fell fast asleep.

"So, what on earth have you gotten yourself in to?" she asked the tiny baby as she sucked the bottle. "You seem a little young to have made enemies, yet there apparently are some really bad people after you." She remembered the man in the uniform. "Or at least one really bad man." She wondered if the man who'd shot the accident survivor was a dirty cop, or if he was an assassin who had stolen a uniform. The man who had been traveling with the baby had told her not to trust anyone, which led her to believe that he knew that whoever was after the baby had connections in high places.

Once the baby fell asleep, she tucked her under the covers and then got up and took a look around the room. She needed a plan that included something other than just sitting around waiting for the man to find them. She wasn't even sure it was safe to stay in the room until morning, although taking the baby out into the chilly night air wasn't an option either, so she supposed her best bet was to hunker down and wait for sunrise. The question was, what then?

She didn't have her phone, ID, wallet, credit or bank card. The man in the car had said to trust no one, but she did have people in her life she knew she could trust. Her mother, grandmother, and four sisters would all help her in a minute, but she didn't want to drag any of them into whatever was going on until she figured out exactly *what* was going on. The man in the CHP uniform had taken her registration, but the address on it was that of her apartment in San Diego. Still, the man had her name, and she was afraid that once he figured out who she was, he would be able to backtrack and find her family in Minnesota, so perhaps she should warn them. The problem was that she didn't know how to warn them without worrying them.

She paced around the room as she tried to work out her options. Thinking of her family made her think of her hometown, Moosehead, and there was one person there she could trust who would have the skill set necessary to do whatever he had to in this situation. Ben Holiday was a private investigator and an ex-cop. He had moved to Moosehead after she had moved away and was married to an old high-school friend of hers, Holly Thompson. Or at least she had been Holly Thompson before she married the handsome PI, opened a foster care home, and built a family. Harper had met Ben three years ago, while she was living in San Diego. He'd been hired to track down a missing teenager who'd last been seen near Coronado Island. Holly knew that she lived in the area and suggested that Ben contact her for help with the search. In the end, she had helped him track down the missing teen and, in the process, made a lifelong friend.

The more Harper thought about it, the more she realized that contacting Ben was her best bet. Now she just needed to figure out how to get in touch with him without a phone. A quick search of the room confirmed that there wasn't one in it, but maybe the office? The electricity had been off, but the gas had been left on, so perhaps the phone had been left on as well. It would make sense the phone would remain in service so that anyone who called the motel unaware that it was closed for the season could leave a message on an answering machine, which, she bet, was the sort of messaging system this old motel would use.

She walked over to the bed to check on the baby, who was still asleep next to the puppy. Making a quick decision, she grabbed her pocket knife and flashlight and then headed out into the cold night air. The motel office was just off the highway, so she knew she'd need to be careful not to be seen, but while this area was popular with hikers and campers during the summer, the place would be all but deserted on a cold night in February.

She had just left the shelter of the room at the back of the lot and had started across the pavement when a set of headlights appeared from the south. She quickly ducked behind a large redwood, where she waited until the car drove by. When it had passed, she continued toward the office and café. She was just passing the gas pumps when another set of headlights appeared on the horizon. Apparently, she'd been wrong about the place being deserted. She ducked behind one of the pumps and watched as a CHP vehicle slowed and then pulled into the lot. She froze as the car stopped in front of the motel office. A tall man got out and walked over to the door. It wasn't the same one she had seen shoot the two car accident victims, but not knowing who to trust, she stayed put. The man knocked on the door, then tried the lock. He shone his flashlight around, missing her hiding spot by inches. He walked back to the car and then pulled out a handheld radio. "Redwood Junction is clear. The place is locked up tight and there is no sign of the driver of the vehicle or the baby. I'll continue to keep my eyes open. They can't have gotten far unless the driver managed to hitch a ride."

He took one last look around, got into his car, and drove away. She let out the breath she'd been holding since he pulled into the lot. She figured she was safe for now, but come daylight, it would be a different story altogether. After making sure there were no other headlights in either direction, she ran to the front door of the motel office. She quickly picked the lock and slipped inside. She knew she couldn't risk a light, even the one from the flashlight, so she felt around until she found the desk where she suspected she'd find the phone. She let out a long sigh of relief when she got a dial tone. She momentarily wondered whether using the phone might somehow give away her location, but right now she needed a way out of this mess, so she took a chance and dialed the familiar number.

She listened as the line was answered by a recording. "You have reached Holiday Investigations. We are currently unavailable or on another line, but if you leave your name and number, someone will call you back."

"Ben, this is Harper Hathaway. I need help. Don't call my cell or text or try to reach me using any of my known contact information. I'm going to try your cell. If that doesn't work, I'll try back in a half hour."

She hung up and then dialed Ben's cell.

"Harper, I just got your message. I was hoping you'd try the cell. What's going on?"

She explained about the accident, the baby, the warning issued by the man in the car, and the uniformed officer who had shot him.

"Wow." Ben paused. "I'm not sure what to say. I can't imagine what is going on that would cause a highway patrolman to shoot a man and a woman in cold blood."

"There was a thumb drive in the diaper bag that might explain what is going on, but I don't have a way to read it. I'm not sure what to do. I don't have transportation, ID, or money, and the man who was driving the car with the baby said not to trust anyone. After seeing a man in uniform shoot him and the woman with him with my own eyes, I'm hesitant to call 9-1-1. I don't think that staying here is an option. The highway patrol seemed to be checking on the place. It is cold and damp and I am traveling with a puppy and an infant. I need help and I need it fast."

Ben paused for a moment before replying. "I have a friend, Michael Maddox. He is a tech wiz and we have worked together on a few cases. He is actually in California this month, setting up a security system for a financial planning firm. I'm going to give him a call. If he is still in the same location he was when I last spoke to him, he should be able to get to you in five or six hours."

She let out a sigh of relief. "That would be great."

"Since I can't call you, how about you call me back in thirty minutes?"

Chapter 2

Michael Maddox pulled into the lot at his hotel. He'd been in California for a month now and was beginning to feel the tug in his chest calling him home. Not that he really minded that his job as a cybersecurity consultant and software developer took him all over the world, but after this long on the road, he always felt the urge to head back to Minnesota. Today was his last day on this particular job, so it wouldn't be long before he would be able to leave the temperate climate of Central California for the subzero temperatures in the north.

With the completion of this job, he would basically be unemployed for the next six weeks. He was sure he could rustle something up if he really wanted to work, but it had been a while since he'd had time to relax. Maybe he'd take some time off to enjoy the rest of the winter. It had been eons since he'd gone ice fishing. Maybe he'd call his friend, Ben Holiday. It had been forever since the two of them had taken a guys' trip. Of course, Michael acknowledged, Ben was a busy man. Not only was he married to a popular advice columnist who traveled for work almost as often as he did, but the couple had built a blended family consisting of biological, adopted, and foster children that appeared to keep him on his toes.

He turned off the ignition and was beginning to gather his belongings when his phone rang. He answered without bothering to check his caller ID. "Maddox here."

"Michael, it's Megan."

Michael smiled at the sound of his middle sister's voice. "Meg, how are you?"

"Busy. I only have a minute, but I wanted to call to make sure you've made your travel reservations."

"Travel reservations?"

"Mom and Dad's anniversary. You do remember? You promised."

He did remember, although for the life of him, he'd been trying to forget. "I know I promised, but I'm in California on a job. It's taking longer than I anticipated. I don't think I'm going to make it back in time."

"Not making it back is not an option," Megan insisted in a stern voice. "Neither Macy nor Marley are going to make it back, which means that it is up to you and me."

Michael winced. He felt bad about missing his parents' anniversary party yet again, but he really, really didn't want to go home.

"Please, Michael." He couldn't help but hear the desperation in her voice. "I'm counting on you to be there."

"You know how busy I am," Michael tried.

"Really?" He could hear the desperation turn to anger. "You are going to use the *I'm busy* excuse with your younger sister, who is not only doing a demanding surgical rotation as part of her pediatric residency at one of the most demanding hospitals in the country but is applying for jobs at every major hospital in the world and is planning the entire party by herself?"

Michael groaned. She had him there. "Okay. I'm sorry. I'll be home. I promise. Will it just be you and me and Mom and Dad?"

"No. Matthew and Julia will be there as well."

Michael didn't reply. Despite Megan's efforts to keep the family together, it seemed as if there had been one obstacle after another. First there was Maddie, and then there was Julia. Totally different situations, but family dividers all the same.

"I know that Matthew attending the party is the real reason you don't want to come," Megan continued. "And I know you have a good reason to want to avoid him, but this isn't about you. It is about finding a way to be a family despite our challenges, and the parents who sacrificed a lot while we were growing up so that we could follow our dreams as adults."

Michael hung his head. "I know. I'm sorry. I'll make the reservations tonight. I'll call you later with the details."

"Thanks." Megan sighed in relief. "I know this is difficult for you."

"It's not difficult," Michael lied. "In fact, I'm totally over it. So, how is the job hunt going?" He wanted desperately to move the subject away from his twin brother and ex-fiancée.

"Slowly. I am more than qualified for every job I have applied for. And I have excellent references. The problem is, the other applicants who have applied for those same jobs are equally qualified. Maybe even more qualified. I have to admit that I am beginning to become discouraged. I really hoped to have a job to go to when my residency is finished in May."

"It sounds tough, but I know the perfect job is waiting for you. Maybe you just haven't stumbled across it."

"I love your optimism, but I don't think my lack of 'stumbling' is the reason I haven't even been granted an interview." Meg groaned. "Perhaps I should lower my standards. I really thought I would be able to snag one of the elite jobs I've always dreamed of, but elite jobs attract elite candidates, and there are a lot more of them than I ever imagined."

"Hang in there, sis. The perfect job is out there."

"Easy for you to say. You've somehow managed to do a wonderful job of stumbling your way through life without so much as the beginnings of a plan. I, on the other hand, have adhered to a rigid set of goals and objectives since I was a teenager, and where has it gotten me?"

"A residency at one of the best hospitals in the country."

Meg laughed. "I guess you are right. Enough with the whining. I'm really looking forward to seeing you. We all are. Maybe as long as you're home for mom and dad's anniversary you can just stay through Christmas."

"I said I'd come home for the anniversary party, but I never said I'd stay through Christmas."

"I know but I miss you."

"I miss you as well." Michael looked at the screen when his cell beeped. "Listen, I have to go. Ben Holiday is on the other line."

"You'll make the reservations? Tonight?"

"I will. I promise."

"Don't let me down, big bro. I'm counting on you."

"I'll be there with bells on. Love you."

"Love you too."

Michael hung up with Megan and answered Ben's call. "I was just thinking about you."

"You were?"

Michael glanced at the first drops of rain as they landed on his windshield. "I've finished up here and am planning to head home in the next day or two. Are you up for some ice fishing?"

"I am. But first I need a favor. A big favor."

Chapter 3

Harper headed back to check on the baby while she waited. She let herself out of the office door, locked it behind her just in case, then paused, considering the small café. It was closed for the season, but they may have left something behind. If nothing else, she wanted to find something for the puppy. She pulled out her knife, picked one more lock, and slipped inside. She headed to the kitchen to find that the cabinets were bare with the exception of a few canned items. When she came across a can of SPAM, she figured that would work for the puppy, so she grabbed it, along with a can of peaches, then slipped out of the café, locked the door, and sprinted across the dark lot toward the room where she'd left the sleeping dog and infant.

"I have food," she said to the pup, who raised his head and wagged his tail when she came in. The baby was still sleeping peacefully, so she used her knife to open both the SPAM and the peaches. The pup inhaled the food without even stopping to chew and then jumped back onto the bed, curled up with the baby, and went back to sleep. She plucked one of the peaches from the heavy syrup and nibbled on it, but her appetite was pretty much nonexistent, so she set the can aside. She wasn't sure what she was going to do if Ben's friend was no longer in the area, or if he was unable to help her for some reason. Both her experience in the Army and her life as a scuba diver and treasure hunter had taught her to think on her feet no matter the situation. And she was good at doing just that, in most cases. But in most cases, she didn't have a baby and a puppy to think about.

She drew the curtains closed except for a small sliver she could peek through. Shutting out the natural light provided by the moon made the room even darker, but she had no way of knowing if the patrolman who had been by earlier would come back again and she wasn't taking any chances. She knew that it was vital to any good plan to have an escape route. She'd chosen the room on the end, which had a small window in the bathroom the others didn't appear to have. It would be a tight squeeze to get herself, the baby, and the puppy through the narrow opening, but if push came to shove, that was exactly what she would do.

She took the thumb drive out of her pocket and looked at it. She didn't have her computer or any other way to read it, but she felt it might be the key to what had been going on with the people in the car. There was an ancient computer in the office, but without electricity to run it, it did her little good.

She froze as a car pulled into the lot. She crossed the room and peeked out the window. It was a dark-colored minivan. Chances were, it belonged to a passing motorist who'd remembered the small travel stop and hoped to find gas or lodging. The van sat in the lot for two or three minutes before continuing on.

Harper didn't have her phone or a watch, so she had no way to keep track of time, but after she assumed thirty minutes could have passed, she checked on the baby and the puppy, both of whom were still asleep, and let herself out of the room to go back to the office. She picked up the phone and dialed Ben's number.

"Everything is set," he said as soon as he answered. "Michael was just getting back to his hotel when I called. He is going to grab a few things and will be on the road heading in your direction within half an hour. The traffic should be light at this time of night, so he estimates he should reach you in about six hours. He won't be able to call you, but I am going to give you his cell number so you can check in with him if you'd like."

"Okay, great." She rooted around for a pen and paper and took down the number.

"It's nine o'clock now, so look for him at around three."

"What make, model, and color car will he be driving?"

"Black Range Rover with Minnesota plates."

"Okay, I'll look for him. And thanks, Ben. I don't know what I would do if you couldn't help. I'm usually pretty good at taking care of myself, but with an infant and a puppy, I'm afraid I'm a bit out of my depth."

"How is the baby?"

"She seems okay, which is amazing because she can't be more than a few days old and was just involved in a serious accident. The car seat she was strapped into was a good one, and the car didn't look as if it had rolled, which may be why she appears to be unharmed."

"Is she eating?"

"She is. She is not a fan of a cold bottle, but the gas is still on, so I used hot tap water to warm it."

She listened as Ben let out a breath. "That's good. I'll feel better once Michael gets there. He is a good guy and you can trust him. The fact that a CHP officer seems to be involved in whatever is going on has me worried, but I guess we'll just take things one challenge at a time until we can work things through."

"It will be fine," she said, even though she didn't necessarily believe it. "I should get back to the room to check on the baby."

"Before you go, I want you to describe the highway patrolman you saw shoot the occupants of the vehicle. I'm going to see if I can track down his identity."

"Tall. Over six feet. Short dark hair. Thin. Crooked nose, which looked to have been broken in the past." Harper paused and thought about him. "I didn't get a real close look so I can't tell you his eye color. I guess the crooked nose is the best clue I can provide."

"Okay. I'll see what I can find out. Be careful and check in when you can."

She rang off, then slipped out of the office and went back to the room where she'd left the baby and puppy. The puppy looked as if he wanted to go out, so she took a quick peek at the baby, who was still sleeping, and took him out behind the building in case a car came down the road. She really, really hoped that the highway patrol wouldn't be back, but she had no way of knowing when or if they would.

The puppy did his thing and she took him back to the room, then tried to get some rest. She fed and changed the baby again at around eleven o'clock. After the baby settled down and went back to sleep, she took the puppy out one more time, then laid down beside both of them. She'd tucked the baby in next to her chest, and the puppy settled on her other side. She was sure the baby would be warm despite the fact that the room was not heated. She must have fallen asleep at some point, although she'd intended to stay awake. When she noticed headlights shining in through the window, she assumed it was Michael Maddox. She got up and peeked out of the small opening in the curtain and almost had a heart attack when she saw it was a CHP vehicle. She could only hope whoever had stopped by would take a quick look around and drive on.

She kept the drapes drawn, so other than the small crack visible between them, she couldn't see much. She looked at the pup, who had started to growl. "Don't bark," she ordered, then glanced at the bathroom behind her. The baby was still asleep, but if the pup barked, he would give them away for sure. She gently picked up the baby, grabbed the diaper bag, called softly to the puppy, and moved everyone to the bathroom. She closed the door except for a narrow crack she could peek through. She could hear whoever had gotten out of the car knocking on and then jiggling the handle of every door. Had she locked the room door the last time she took the puppy out?

She heard the knock on their door and waited for the jiggle before she heard another car pull up. The man who had been checking doors seemed to have walked away because she heard him greet whoever had just arrived. She couldn't hear what was being said, but after a few minutes, she heard both vehicles drive away. She waited where she was for several minutes, then slowly opened the bathroom door. She hadn't heard anything since the vehicles had pulled away and was about to sneak over to the window for a quick look when the door opened to reveal a tall, broad-shouldered man dressed in dark clothing.

Chapter 4

"Harper Hathaway?"

Her heart raced as she struggled not to panic. She tightened her arms around the baby. The puppy, who had been able to control his instinct to bark until this moment, let loose with a chorus of vicious barking and growling.

"You can call off your attack dog. I'm Michael Maddox. Ben sent me."

She let out the breath she'd been holding.

"You really should have had your door locked," Michael scolded.

She nodded. "I should have. I must have forgotten after I took the puppy out. The cop?"

"Left to check the couple with car trouble I reported. I pulled away when he did, then circled back."

"There's a couple driving on this road at this time of the night?"

"No, there isn't. We need to go."

She nodded. All she had was the baby, the puppy, and the diaper bag, so it didn't take long to gather everything together. It would be light in a couple of hours. She just hoped they were well out of California before then.

"I sent the CHP officer south, which is the direction from which I arrived. Still, we could pass him again, so I am going to suggest that you lay down in the back seat."

"Okay. Whatever you say. I can't tell you how grateful I am."

Michael grabbed a blanket and a pillow from the bed. He put the diaper bag and the puppy in the cargo area, then had her lay down on the back seat with the baby nestled between her body and the back of the seat. He put the pillow under her head and covered them both with the blanket. She hadn't meant to go to sleep, but the next thing she knew, the car was stopping and the sun was high in the sky.

"Where are we?" she asked.

"Oregon. There is a hotel with family suites that I have stayed in a few times. I thought we'd stop and regroup before we go on."

That sounded like a wonderful idea to her. She was sure it was past the baby's feeding time, and the puppy needed to be fed and walked as well.

"I understand that you found a thumb drive in the diaper bag."

She sat up, pulling the baby into her lap. "Yes. I didn't have a way to look at it, so I have no idea what is on it."

"I have my computer. Wait here and I'll see if I can get us a room."

Harper smiled at the baby, who was wide awake now. She looked alert, even happy, which provided her a huge sense of relief. She'd been so worried about the little girl and the previous day's grand adventure, but now that Michael had come to the rescue, she felt certain that they'd be fine.

"The room is in the back," Michael said, getting back into the driver's seat. He started the car and pulled around to the back of the building. The room he had paid for was a suite that included two bedrooms, a seating area, and a kitchenette overlooking the sea.

"Wow, this is beautiful."

"It's one of the best views along this stretch of coast," Michael agreed. "Why don't you see to the baby? I'll take the pup out and then I'll take him with me into town to grab a few supplies. I think we should be safe for now, but as soon as I leave, I want you to secure the privacy lock behind me. Don't open the door for anyone unless you hear me with the safe word."

"Safe word?"

"Pumpernickel. It isn't a word that comes up often in everyday conversation, yet it is easy to remember. If you hear me knock three times and then say 'pumpernickel,' you can open the door. Otherwise keep it locked."

"Pumpernickel. Got it."

"I'm going to grab us some breakfast while I'm out. Any food allergies or aversions?"

She shook her head. "Anything would be great. The pup will need something to eat too."

"I'll grab some dog food, a leash and collar, a dog bed, and maybe a couple of toys while I'm out. Does the baby need anything?"

"She has food and diapers that will last for a few days, but she'll need a car seat and maybe an adjustable infant carrier she can sleep in."

"I'll see if I can find a store that sells baby supplies. I might be an hour or more. Do you need anything?"

"A toothbrush and toothpaste would be great, and maybe a hairbrush. When I fled the scene of the accident, I couldn't take anything with me."

"Okay, I'll see what I can do. Remember to lock the door behind me."

After Michael left with the puppy, she changed the baby and then warmed up a bottle of formula in the microwave. She clicked on the gas fireplace, then settled onto the sofa that was arranged so both the fire and the view could be enjoyed and fed the baby. She really was a beautiful little thing. Tons of dark hair and dark eyes. As she watched the baby eat, she wondered once again about the events that might have led the mother of the baby, as well as her traveling companion, to be shot by a man dressed as an officer of the law. From the visits from the other CHP officers while she was hiding at the motel, she had to believe that there was more going on than the involvement of a single rogue cop. As she stared into the eyes of the baby in her arms, her heart filled with love. The man in the driver's seat had told her to keep the baby safe, and in that moment, she knew she would die doing just that if it came down to it.

By the time the baby had been fed and tucked in for a nap, Michael returned with the puppy. He had armloads of supplies, so she entertained the pup while he unloaded everything. Not only had he purchased a quality car seat and infant carrier for the baby but, as promised, the pup had been outfitted with puppy food, bowls, toys, a bed, and a leash and collar.

Michael handed her a bag. "I bought some toiletries as well as a clean pair of sweatpants, a T-shirt, and a sweatshirt that I hope will fit you. We can stop somewhere later so you can pick out some things that are more to your liking, but for now, I figured sweats would be the most size neutral."

She accepted the bag. "Thank you so much. I'd love to take a shower and get cleaned up a bit. I have mud on my jeans from my trip down the embankment at the scene of the accident and spit-up on my shoulder from the baby."

"I brought us breakfast." Michael held up another bag. "Let's eat first and then I'll take a look at the thumb drive and check in with Ben while you clean up."

Now that, she thought, sounded like a wonderful plan. The breakfast sandwiches were hot and cheesy and the coffee was exactly what she needed to feel halfway human again.

"Ben said that your family lives in Moosehead."

She nodded. "I, along with my four sisters, were born and raised there. In fact, the Hathaways have lived in Moosehead for three generations."

"I wasn't aware that Moosehead had even been a town for three generations."

"I guess it hasn't been incorporated for that long, but my grandmother, Dixie, has lived on Hathaway land for more than fifty years."

Michael raised a brow. "Impressive. Was her father a farmer?"

"No, Dixie moved to Moosehead on her own when she was in her early twenties. She was and continues to be a real character who was firmly entrenched in the hippie movement of the sixties. She met my grandfather, Denver Hathaway, while visiting the area in the early sixties, and in 1963, my mother,

Daisy, was born. I don't think that my grandparents planned for or even particularly wanted a child then, but my mother was loved and nurtured from her first moment of life. Eventually, the women's movement and political activism kicked in as the seventies took hold, and many of the residents of the commune where Dixie and Denver lived had moved on to other things. In 1976, Denver bought out the owners of the property and settled in with Dixie to raise both crops and a family. Unfortunately, by the time Dixie and Denver decided they wanted to have more children, my mother was already thirteen and Dixie was past her prime childbearing years.

Michael seemed interested in her story and it provided a distraction, so she continued. "In 1984, my mother, who is a veterinarian and, currently, the mayor of Moosewood, met my father, a freelance carpenter and rock and roll guitarist ten years her senior, Jagger Oswald. In 1985, my older sister, Hayden, was born. I came along two years later, and during the course of the next eight years, my three younger sisters arrived. Although my parents had five daughters together and seemed to love each other very much, they never did get around to getting married. My mom, being a product of her own free-loving mother, made a deal with my father when Hayden was born: all the girls born from their union would carry her last name and all the boys would carry his. Poor Papa died sixteen years ago without leaving a single male offspring to carry on his name, but his memory and his gift for music, has been carried on by all his daughters."

Michael chuckled. "Wow. That is a very complete family history."

She shrugged. "I figured if we are going to be traveling together, we might as well get to know each other. How about you? Your SUV has Minnesota license plates. Do you live in Moosehead?"

"Minneapolis, although to be honest, I am rarely there. I own a cybersecurity firm and travel a lot for work."

"So, if you don't live in Moosehead, how do you know Ben?"

Michael took a sip of his coffee. "Ben and I met when we both lived in New York. He was a cop at the time, and I was a hacker who enjoyed bending the rules in the name of fun and games. To be honest, I was young and stupid and managed to get myself wrapped up with a pretty bad group of people. Ben arrested me for illegal hacking, which turned out to be a good thing. We got to know each other, and he convinced me to use my superpower for good rather than evil. Eventually, he quit the force, moved to Moosehead, and opened a PI firm. After a couple of years, he married a local girl and had a bunch of kids. I was working in home security by that time, and after Ben got settled, he encouraged me to start my own company. We've worked together on a few of his cases, and I had visited Moosehead on several occasions, so when the time came for me to leave New York, I decided to move to Minneapolis to be close to Ben, who had become sort of a mentor for me."

"If you wanted to move closer to Ben, why not Moosehead?"

Michael lifted a shoulder. "Moosehead was a little too remote for my taste. At least it was when I first made the move. Now, however, I'm not sure. I travel a lot for business and Minneapolis is convenient as a home base. Still, I will admit that when I see what Ben has, I sometimes find myself daydreaming about settling down with my own house on Beaver Lake." Michael looked at her. "Ben mentioned that you hadn't been home in quite a long time. I guess you found Moosehead to be too remote for you as well?"

She nodded. "I couldn't wait to get out of there after high school, so I joined the Army when I was eighteen and haven't been back since."

"But you were on your way back when you found the baby?"

She nodded. "I was. After I left the Army, I traveled the world scuba diving one exotic location after another with the man who became my fiancé. It was during one of those trips that he died while diving on a wreck. After he was gone, I realized that I wanted something different in life. I honestly have no idea what I am going to do now, but I knew I didn't want to stay in California, so I packed my bags with the intention of finally going home. I'd decided on the scenic route north, which, as it turned out, might have been a mistake." She thought about the baby. "No. Not a mistake. I think it was fate that I was the one who happened across the accident. Someone else might have simply called 9-1-1 and the baby might have met with the same fate as her mother."

Michael got up and tossed his fast-food wrapper in the trash. "Which brings us to the reason someone is after the baby." He picked up his laptop and set it on the dining table. "If you have that thumb drive, we can take a look."

She pulled the drive out of her pocket and handed it to Michael. He inserted it into his computer and waited for it to open.

"It's password protected."

"Can you get in?"

Michael nodded. "It might take some time, but I'll get in."

She stood up and tossed her trash as well. "I'm going to jump in the shower. The baby has been fed and is sleeping. I don't think she will wake up, but if she does, there are diapers in the diaper bag. Do you know how to change a diaper?"

Michael chuckled. "I'm not sure I've actually ever changed one, but I think I can manage."

"Okay, great. I'll hurry." After heating up the bathroom, she stepped under the spray of hot water. She simply stood under the powerful showerhead as she willed the tension in her back and shoulders to dissipate. Had it really been only twenty-four hours since she'd left San Francisco? It seemed as if it was days ago. She supposed at some point she was going to have to call her mother. She'd be expecting her. Although her mother knew that she planned to drive from San Diego to Moosehead, and they'd talked about her interest in taking the scenic route rather than hopping on the interstate, so she most likely wouldn't begin to worry if she hadn't heard from her for several days at least.

Michael had purchased both shampoo and conditioner appropriate for her hair type. After she washed and rinsed her hair twice, she soaped up her body, then did a final rinse before turning off the water and grabbing one of the thick, fluffy towels the hotel provided.

Michael looked up when she returned to the sitting area wearing her new sweats. "It looks like they fit."

She nodded. "The sweats are very comfortable. Did you get into the thumb drive?"

"Not yet, but I will. I did check in with Ben. He wants you to call him." Michael handed her a burner phone. "Use this. Ben said to call this number." Michael handed her a phone number that he'd written down on a napkin. "Ben is going to use a burner as well. He said not to call the office or his cell from this point. I think the fact that the California Highway Patrol seems to be involved in whatever is going on has him worried."

"Yeah," she said, sitting down on the sofa. "It has me worried too." She glanced at the computer. "I just hope there is something on that drive that can help us make sense of all this." She used the burner to dial the number he'd given her.

Ben picked up after the first ring. "I'm glad to see that you made it out of California all right."

"Yeah," she agreed. "Me too. Things were pretty dicey there for a while, but Michael seems to have things under control. He's checked us into a hotel using his name only, so no one even knows I'm with him. Well, no one *should* know I am. Do you have any idea what is going on?"

"No," Ben admitted. "I did track down your shooter. Or at least I think I did. His name is Curt Loughlin. He has been with the CHP for twelve years and, as far as I can tell, has never been the subject of disciplinary action. I can't explain why he shot the man and the woman in the car in cold blood, but given your description and his photo, I assume we are discussing the same man."

"Can you email a photo to Michael?"

"Yeah. Hang on."

She waited for Ben to come back on the line. The scenario was completely bizarre.

"Okay," Ben said. "Have Michael check his email."

He did and she nodded. "Yep, that's him," she confirmed. "The fact that this guy is involved has me worried. Do you think he acted alone, or could there be other members of the CHP involved?"

"I don't know. I want you to walk me through everything that happened."

She took a deep breath and blew it out slowly. "All right. I was heading north up the coast and had just passed the point where the coastal view gives way to the redwoods when a dog ran in front of my car. I slammed on the brakes and swerved to avoid him. I managed to bring the car to a stop and avoid hitting the animal, but the car was in bad shape because I drove into a drainage ditch. I got out and went to look for the dog, who is really no more than a puppy. I hadn't thought I'd hit him, but I wanted to be sure. It was the dog that led me to a blue sedan that looked as if it had been run off the road. The male passenger was unconscious when I first arrived, but when I checked his pulse, he came to. He told me to hide the baby, who was strapped into a car seat in the back seat of the vehicle. There was also a female passenger, but the driver told me she was dead. I grabbed the baby and the diaper bag and was trying to figure out what to do next when I heard another vehicle on the highway. I guess it was instinct that made me hide rather than greet the patrolman who climbed down from the road to the car. I thought he might help the driver, but instead he pulled out a gun and shot him. He also shot the passenger, who I assume was the baby's mother, but like I said, it seemed she was already dead. It looked as if she had suffered a gunshot wound to the chest before the accident."

"And after he shot the occupants of the vehicle?"

"He pulled out a phone and called someone. He said that Agent Beaverton was dead and so was the witness. He also informed the person on the other end of the line that the baby was gone, and he suspected that whoever had been in the car in the ditch, which was mine, had probably taken it. Then he climbed back up to the road and took my purse, phone, and vehicle registration from my car."

"Anything else?" Ben asked.

"He assured the person on the phone that he'd find them one way or another. I assumed he meant the baby and the driver of the abandoned vehicle." Harper frowned. "Wait, there was something else. He made a comment about 'the ledger' being missing."

"Did you find a ledger?"

"No. All I took from the vehicle was the baby and the diaper bag."

"You said you found a thumb drive in the diaper bag. Are you sure there wasn't a ledger in there too?"

"I emptied out the bag when I was looking for diapers and formula. If there had been anything as large as a ledger, I would have seen it immediately. Maybe Agent Beaverton hid it before he set out with the woman and the baby. Or maybe the ledger is on the thumb drive. Michael is working on getting into it right now."

"After the man in the uniform left, what did you do?"

"I walked down the road with the dog and the baby until I came to a little tourist stop. It was closed for the season, but I picked the lock on one of the motel rooms and then called you. After I fed and changed the baby and got the puppy settled I called you and then waited for Michael to come and rescue us. I wonder who Agent Beaverton was."

"I don't know, but I'll find out. I know I've said this before, but I'm going to say it again: I'm really not liking this one bit."

"Tell me about it."

"Is the baby still doing well?"

"She seems to be doing fine. She is eating, her color is good, and she seems healthy."

"I'm glad to hear that. We are going to stay in constant contact until we get this resolved using the burner phones only. Don't call anyone but me using the phone Michael gave you. We will change out the phones we use every couple of calls to avoid detection. I want you to lay low. If Michael can access the thumb drive, we might be able to figure out who is behind everything that has happened, and if you find a ledger of some sort, I suspect we'll know a lot more. In the meantime, get some rest. There is a good chance you'll need to move again sooner rather than later."

She glanced out the window at the beautiful view. It looked like any normal day. It really was too bad that it wasn't. "Okay. And if you find out anything, let us know."

"I will. Have you told anyone other than Michael and me what's happened to you? Your family?"

"No. Just you. I don't want to drag them into this."

"That's good. I'm going to do some digging. I'll check back in with you both in a couple of hours."

She hung up and looked at Michael, who was still hard at work. It had been several hours since the baby had eaten and the puppy had been out. She decided to check on the baby, and if she was still asleep, she'd take the puppy for a bathroom break. Despite the fact that she was in a beautiful hotel with a handsome man, she couldn't wait for this whole thing to be over so she could go home.

"I'll take the puppy out for a quick run on the beach," she said to Michael once she'd seen the baby, who was still asleep.

"I'll take him. You should stay out of sight until we know whether anyone is following us."

"Do you think someone is?" she asked. "I hoped that once we crossed the state line we'd be out of danger."

"Given the circumstances that brought us here, I don't think that the state line is going to offer us any protection. The man who shot the occupants of the car took your wallet, which I assume held your ID. They know who you are and what you look like."

Michael had a point. Loughlin did have her photo ID. She supposed she should stay in the room despite how lovely a day it appeared to be. "Okay, I guess you are right. I'll stay here with the baby while you take the puppy out."

Michael clipped on the leash. "Do you think we should name him? The pup? It looks like he is going to be traveling with us."

"I guess. I'm also getting tired of calling the baby, *the baby*. I thought that maybe her name would be mentioned on the thumb drive, so I have avoided coming up with my own name for her."

"What about a nickname?"

"That would work. How about Princess? My dad called me Princess Rose when I was little because my middle name is Rose. In fact, he had nicknames for all five of us. My older sister Hayden was Kiwi, and Haley was Jellybean."

"I think Princess is a great nickname for the baby until we can figure out what her actual name is. And the puppy?"

"How about Bosley? I had a lab named Bosley when I was a kid. Best dog ever."

"Bosley it is." Michael opened the door. "I'll just be a few minutes, but latch the privacy lock just in case."

Chapter 5

Michael let the puppy off the leash as soon as they'd made it through the parking lot to the deserted beach. The last time he'd been here had been Christmas two years ago. He'd been avoiding his family, so he'd purposely taken a job in Portland that he'd sworn to his mother would keep him occupied from the twentieth of December until after the New Year. Of course, the job hadn't even started until after January 1, so he'd checked into his hotel in Portland and then driven down the coast in search of a peaceful location to lick his wounds. At the time, he'd been so miserable that he hadn't enjoyed the scenery, but with time had come a healing of his damaged heart, and he'd found that he enjoyed the steady rhythm of the waves rolling onto the sand.

He picked up a stick and tossed it for the dog, thinking about the woman waiting back at the hotel. Julia's betrayal had deadened his heart so completely that it had been years since he'd felt the slightest attraction for anyone, beyond the random physical pull he couldn't help but experience when encountering a beautiful woman. He had to admit that in the few hours he'd known her, Harper's bravery and willingness to do whatever was necessary to protect the dog, and then the baby had penetrated his stone-cold heart in a way he wasn't quite sure he was ready to deal with. She had, he reminded himself, recently lost her fiancé. He doubted she would be ready to enter into another romantic relationship for a good long time. It was important to his own well-being that he remember that. Keeping her at arm's length really did seem to be the best plan because he was sure his heart couldn't take another hit so soon.

Thinking of Julia made him sad. God, he had loved the woman who had professed to love him back. He'd never been the sort to settle down until he met the blond vixen with huge green eyes, pouty lips, and a giving energy that had grabbed hold of his heart from the first day he'd met her. He'd worked hard after Ben had arrested him, and after years of sacrifice, he'd finally felt he had something to offer a woman. He'd owned a beautiful apartment in the city and owned and operated his own business. He'd fallen deeply in love with Julia within hours of meeting her and had been so sure that she was the one he was destined to spend his life with. And he would have. He was certain of that. He would have forged ahead and never looked back if Matthew hadn't come home from an overseas teaching assignment just weeks before they were to be married. It had taken a single look from the man who looked exactly like him but was very much different in terms of personality, to sweep the love of his life off her feet, destroying his life in the process.

Bosley dropped the stick at his feet, dancing around for him to toss it again. He picked it up and threw it as hard as he could. The puppy sure was a cute little thing. He couldn't help but wonder whether he'd been with Agent Beaverton, the dead woman, and the baby. Michael frowned. It bothered him more than he wanted to admit that someone might be after the infant, wishing to do her harm. What sort of monster would want to hurt a baby? He and Harper didn't have much to go on yet, but one way or another, he knew he would do whatever it took to keep the baby and the woman who had rescued her safe. His best hope right now to do that was to figure out how to unlock the thumb drive; hopefully, that would lead to the answers they needed to navigate the murky waters into which Harper had been thrust. Calling the puppy to his side, he turned and headed back toward the hotel.

Chapter 6

Harper went into the bathroom to dry her hair after Michael left with Bosley. By the time she had managed to tame her thick brown hair, Princess was awake and had begun to fuss. She headed into the bedroom to change her diaper and grab another bottle. Her sister Harlow loved children and would most likely be in seventh heaven if she were to bring the baby home. Of course, she hadn't spent time with Harlow for a very long time. Perhaps the teenager who loved to babysit even more than she liked to hang out with her friends had grown into a woman too busy for either children or friends. She owned her own bookstore now, which she was certain demanded quite a bit of her time and attention.

The more she thought about it, the more bothered Harper became that she barely knew her sisters anymore. She had missed so much during the fourteen years she'd been away. She'd been overseas doing her second tour of duty when her youngest sister, Haven, graduated high school, and she'd just left US soil for a trip to Australia, where she and Eric had signed on to a salvage operation when her middle sister, Haley, the sister she was probably the closest to, had dropped out of college and moved back to Moosehead after a nasty breakup with the guy she'd dated since middle school. Haley owned her own construction company now and seemed to be doing well, but Harper hadn't been there for her when she needed her most.

Even though her visits with her sisters had been limited to the times they'd come to see her, Harper had tried to stay on top of the important events in their lives. Hayden was a popular on-air reporter for a local television station operating out of the Twin Cities, with dreams of making it big once she landed her dream job at a network, and Haven was a budding artist and musician who worked with their mother at the veterinary practice she had owned since Harper was a baby.

After heating the formula, she snuggled onto the sofa with the baby. Princess stared at her with huge brown eyes, seemingly fixated on her face as she drank. Her heart melted just a bit when Princess looked at her with such serious concentration. To be honest, Harper had never wanted children of her own. She was thirty-two years old now and should be considering that sort of thing, but settling down as the mother of a couple of kids had never been part of either her short- or her long-term plans. If Eric hadn't died and she hadn't lost her will to go on with the life that had suited her when they were a couple, they might very well have continued continent-hopping until they were ready to retire to the old folks' home.

When Michael got back with Bosley, the puppy settled down on the bed he'd bought him with the chew toy he'd also purchased.

"I'm going to pay you back for all the stuff you bought as soon as I can access my bank account," she informed him.

Michael shrugged. "Don't even think about it now. I was happy to help out." He frowned. "I think I am close to being able to get into the thumb drive. I've had a program working in the background that should be just about done."

"I hope there is something useful on the drive because not a single thing that has happened since Bosley ran out into the road in front of my car has made a bit of sense."

It took Michael a bit longer than he expected, but before too long he announced that he was in. Princess had finished her bottle, so Harper set the infant carrier on the table and tucked her in. She seemed content as she looked at the cute bunny mobile Michael had bought. Harper sat down next to him and said, "So, what do we have?"

"There are several files," he answered. "Five in all." He opened the first, which was labeled AGREEMENT.

"What is it?" she asked.

"A contract of some sort. It looks as if someone named Isabella Fernandez has agreed to provide important information to the Drug Enforcement Agency about a man named Salvador Garcia in exchange for US citizenship for her baby, asylum for herself, and a new identity."

"The woman in the car must have been Isabella. Do you have any idea who Salvador Garcia is?"

Michael continued to read. "A powerful drug lord operating out of South America who is currently in the United States. It looks as if the DEA has been after him for a long time, but he's been too smart and too well protected to allow himself to be found and captured." Michael frowned.

"What is it?"

"According to this statement, it appears that Isabella was a teenager living on the streets when she met Garcia. After she became pregnant, she decided she didn't want her baby to be raised by the man who she'd realized had violent tendencies, so when he brought her to the United States for a short visit, she ran. After she escaped Garcia's compound, the girl somehow was able to connect with a police officer and convinced him that she had something to offer in exchange for sanctuary. According to this document, the police officer she had turned to put her in touch with the DEA."

"So, if she made a deal with the DEA, who killed her and why are they after the baby?"

"I don't know. Maybe they aren't after the baby at all. Maybe they are after the thumb drive or the ledger and assume whoever has the baby is in possession of those items as well." Michael opened another file. It contained a video of the man who had been driving the car Harper found, which was also carrying the dead woman and the baby. He identified himself as Agent Beaverton and stated that he had been assigned to guard Isabella Fernandez until she gave birth. Apparently, she had not been willing to provide the DEA with the information they were looking for until after her baby was born. She wanted to ensure the baby's American citizenship by making certain that he or she was born on US soil. The baby was born several hours before the video had been recorded, according to Beaverton's testimony. He took down Isabella's statement, which included the location of a ledger that he assured his superiors would provide all the hard data they needed to find and arrest Garcia.

"Is there any information in the file as to where the ledger is?" Harper asked.

Michael shook his head. "No. I don't think so. There are three more files, though."

He opened the next file, which contained a frantic video made by Beaverton saying that he had received intel that there was a mole in the DEA who was working for Salvador Garcia. According to his source, the life of the witness was in danger. He wanted to be sure there was a record of the agreement that Isabella had with the DEA and his actions upon learning of the leak, which was why he had transferred all pertinent information to the thumb drive. The video indicated that he planned to move the mother and child and would figure out what to do and who to trust once they were safe.

"I guess he never did make it to that safe haven," she said.

"I guess not."

"So, Curt Loughlin, the CHP officer who killed Beaverton, might be working with the mole in the DEA."

"Perhaps. If there is a mole in the DEA, that person might be responsible for the other CHP officers looking for you and the baby. I think that we are going to need to act with even more extreme caution from this point forward. From what I've seen so far, it appears that Salvador Garcia is a powerful man who could very well have moles in other key agencies. I think I have to agree with Beaverton when he said not to trust anyone."

"What is in the other two files?"

Michael opened the fourth file. This one had copies of names, addresses, bank accounts, and other contacts, informants, and information that Garcia was certain to want to keep under wraps. Michael's frown deepened. "I don't think that Garcia would give a second thought to killing anyone he even suspected was threatening to reveal information I am sure he is desperate to see buried. At this point we have no way of knowing if Beaverton sent a copy of the information Isabella provided after delivering her baby to anyone else, but if this is the only copy of that information, it should be considered invaluable."

Fantastic. "If Garcia is the baby's father, why would he want her dead?"

"As I said before, he may not," Michael answered. "He may simply be trying to secure the information the mole most likely told him Isabella planned to turn over to the authorities. If the baby is missing, he may assume the person who has the baby also has the information he is worried about. Still, I don't think we should assume that he is not interested in the baby. Beaverton said to keep her safe and that is what we are going to do."

"What about the last file?"

Michael opened it. "It looks to be some kind of map."

"A map to what?"

Michael frowned. "I'm not sure. Maybe to where the ledger is hidden. I suppose that if Isabella found a way to steal the ledger before she ran away, she may have hidden it."

"Hidden it where?"

Michael shrugged. "I don't know. The map is vague, and the directions included with it appear to have been written in code."

"We know that Isabella was in California. The map must coordinate to a location there."

Michael shook his head. "Isabella was found dead in California, but we don't know where she started out. She could have hidden the ledger anywhere. So far, I'm not sure what state or location the map coordinates with. But given some time, I think we should be able to figure it out. I don't think we should take the time to do that now, though. Staying in one place makes us easier to find should someone pick up our trail."

"So where do we go?"

"I think we head toward Moosehead, but in a nontraditional fashion. We won't want to be predictable. Maybe we head east from here rather than continuing north. I have to assume that if the bad guys have your ID, they eventually will be able to figure out that you might have been driving to Minnesota."

"Do you think my family is in danger?"

Michael appeared to consider her question carefully. "I doubt it, but we'll talk to Ben about keeping an eye on things the next time he calls."

Harper got up and walked over to the window. She would be sad to leave this place. She'd actually felt safe for a few hours. "Ben has a lot of contacts in the FBI and other agencies. Maybe we should get help."

"Maybe. That may be an option we are forced to take. But for now, let's just keep moving while Ben does the detective thing. He might be able to narrow in on exactly who Beaverton and by extension we are dealing with. Once we know that, we'll have a better idea of who to turn to. I'll go out to pick up something to eat, some more diapers and formula, and a few additional supplies for the road."

"You're leaving?"

"For a couple of hours. It could be a long night, so try to get some sleep. And, as before, secure the privacy latch behind me."

Lordy, what had she gotten herself into?

After Michael left, she decided to call Ben. She took out the number of the burner cell Ben had sent to communicate with him and dialed.

"Harper. How are things going?"

"Have you spoken to Michael about the information on the thumb drive?"

"He called to fill me in. I know about the mole in the DEA, Agent Beaverton's role with them, and the ledger. I assume you are planning to go after it. While I agree that obtaining the ledger might be the best way to get Garcia off your back, I continue to be worried. From what I've been able to uncover from here, Salvador Garcia has connections in high places. There is no doubt in my mind that a rogue CHP officer isn't the only law enforcement official he has in his pocket."

"So what are we supposed to do? Run forever?"

"No. Michael isn't wrong that your best bet is to find the ledger that seemingly will lead to the apprehension of the man who appears to be behind everything. My primary concern, though, is to make sure that you and the baby are safe."

"I can take care of myself, but I am worried about the baby. What's going to happen to her? She is so tiny. This shouldn't be happening."

"If the baby was born shortly before Beaverton whisked her and her mother away, then it is possible that you and Michael are the only two people alive to even have seen her. Maybe it would be best to separate the two of you. If the rogue CHP officer has your ID, he will be looking for you, but he may not know for certain that you have her, and I doubt he knows what she looks like."

"Separate us? How?"

Ben paused, as if to consider the situation. "Maybe I should meet you somewhere and bring the baby home with me. Holly and I have foster kids coming and going all the time. No one would give a second look at a new baby in the mix. I know you are taking excellent care of her, but she might be in more danger traveling with you than she would be if you and Michael went on alone."

Ben made a good point, especially if Michael's plan was to find the ledger. If Isabella had hidden it, they could very well be the only people alive with any way to track it down. "All right. As much as I will miss her, I agree that she will be safer with you. How should we go about this?"

"You are now about two thousand miles from Moosehead. I could fly to Portland and meet you there, but it is likely that Garcia will be watching the airports. It will take longer to drive, but I think that might be our best bet. I'm thinking we should meet halfway. Somewhere off the usual route between Moosehead and your current location."

"Okay, I like your plan. I'll talk to Michael and have him call you as soon as he gets back."

Chapter 7

Harper was surprised when Michael got back to the hotel less than an hour later. They ate Chinese food, and then she fed and changed the baby while Michael fed and walked the puppy. When everyone had eaten and was cared for, they loaded up the SUV with the baby snuggled safely in her car seat and the puppy curled up in the dog bed in the cargo area. "Where are we headed?"

"East to Idaho. Once we arrive there, we'll head north on Highway 95 into Montana. We are going to meet Ben in Wolf Point the day after tomorrow. Once we hand Princess off to Ben, we'll focus on tracking down the ledger, which, in my mind, is going to be the only way to be sure Garcia is off your back."

"Maybe he is already off my back. Nothing suspicious has happened since we left California. Maybe Garcia doesn't know about the thumb drive. Maybe now that Isabella is dead, he has simply gone back to work supplying the US with illegal drugs."

The road Michael had chosen to travel east was a backcountry one, with little traffic. In fact, they hadn't passed a single car in almost thirty minutes. "I hope that is true, but my gut tells me that we are a long way from being in the clear."

"Yeah. My gut is telling me that too. When I spoke to Ben today, he said that we should settle on a temporary name for the baby. A name we can use to refer to her in public if need be. He and I agreed it would be best to act as if the baby is ours until we can hand her off to Ben."

"I think that is a good idea. What should we call her, other than Princess, of course?"

Harper turned her head slightly to look at the sleeping infant. "I would say Isabella after her mother, but that doesn't seem like a good idea. I think we should probably name her something with an American flair. Something that starts with a letter other than an *H*."

Michael turned slightly toward her. "You have something against names that begin with the letter *H*?"

"After growing up with Hayden, Harper, Haley, Harlow, and Haven, I think I've had enough of *H* names."

"I get it. I have three sisters: Macy, Megan, and Marley."

She laughed. "Really? You aren't just making that up to make me feel better?"

Michael held up his right hand. "I swear."

"I believe you. So, tell me about Macy, Megan, and Marley. You said you were from New York originally. Do they all still live there?"

Michael sped up to pass a lumber truck. "No. Macy is a pilot, currently running a charter service in Alaska. Megan is a third-year resident at Boston General, and Marley, who graduated college last spring, lives in Italy, where she hopes to find herself."

"Any brothers?"

Michael's mouth tightened. "One. Matthew."

"Does *he* still live in New York?"

"He did until two years ago. He married a woman whose family lives in New Hampshire, so when she wanted to move closer to her parents, he relocated with her."

"That's nice. I've only been to New England once, but I loved every minute of it and plan to go again someday. Are you and Matthew close?"

"Not really."

She was surprised by his answer. "I'm sensing a conflict of some sort, although it is none of my business and I probably shouldn't even ask about it."

"Matthew is my twin, and the woman he married was my fiancée until she met Matthew three years ago and decided that she would rather be married to a teacher who worked close to home than a business owner who was away much of the time. Not that I really blame her. Matthew is perfect for her. Still, it stings a bit, so do you think we can change the subject?"

"Of course. I'm sorry. I'm sure the situation has been very difficult for you. Let's keep thinking of a name for Princess. How about Bella? It could be considered to be short for Isabella."

"I like it. I think it is perfect, although in my mind, she'll always be Princess."

She smiled. "Yeah. She will forever be Princess in my mind as well."

The conversation paused, and, given the awkward dialogue regarding Michael's brother, Harper felt the need to fill the silence. She didn't think talking about their families any more was the best way to go, though, so talking about someone else's family seemed like a wise switch. "I understand that Ben and Holly not only have six foster children and three adopted children, they have two biological children as well."

Michael nodded. "Joe DiMaggio Holiday and Reggie Jackson Holiday."

"I remember him mentioning that he'd named his sons after famous Yankees. They must be three or four by now."

"They will be four on their next birthday."

"Holly and I are the same age, so we were in the same class all through school. I wouldn't say we were best friends, but we hung out some, and I would say I knew her pretty well. I remember that she couldn't wait to get out of Moosehead after graduation, same as me, and we both left the area before the ink on our diplomas was dry. Neither of us had children or families on our mind at the time, and both of us wanted very much to make a name for ourselves. Now here we are, fourteen years later. She is married but has the fantastic career she dreamed of and eleven children, counting the foster kids, while I am still single but without a job or even a prospect of one on the horizon. How did that happen?"

"I guess people's lives evolve along different timelines, even if they start out in the same place. I wouldn't worry too much about not having a job at this moment." Michael glanced at her. "Something tells me that you are destined to do great things."

She was going to respond, but their conversation was interrupted by the ringing of a phone. "Ben?" she asked when Michael picked it up and looked at the caller ID.

"No. It's not the burner phone." Michael answered using Bluetooth. "Maddox here."

"Mr. Maddox, it's Ray."

She remembered that Michael had told her that Ray was the name of the very nice desk clerk at the hotel they'd just stayed in.

"You told me to call you if someone came in looking for a woman with a baby."

"Yes, I did. Was someone there?" Michael asked.

"Yes, sir. A tall man with dark hair and a crooked nose. He asked if a woman with a baby had checked in during the past twenty-four hours. I told him that I hadn't had a woman with a baby check in during the two years I have worked here, which is actually true."

"What was the man wearing?" Michael asked.

"A dark-colored jacket. Black, I think. He had on jeans and dark-colored boots."

"Did you tell him anything other than that no woman with a baby had checked in?"

"No, sir. I didn't say a word."

"Excellent. You did well, Ray. Very well."

"Happy I helped. It's not every day someone gives me a five-hundred-dollar tip. It is going to come in real handy. Thank you again."

Michael hung up and then turned to glance at her. "It sounds like the man who stopped by the hotel fits the description of Loughlin, the CHP officer who shot Beaverton."

"Except for him wearing street clothes and not a uniform, the description fits exactly. Should we be worried?"

"Probably not. He's most likely going to continue up the coast until he hits Highway 90, if he has indeed decided that you were heading for Moosehead. If we were actually going straight there, that is the route we'd be taking. Even if he hasn't uncovered the Moosehead connection yet, the road we are traveling is not one anyone but a local homeowner would be likely to travel. I think we are safe for now. Still, the visit from the shooter does demonstrate that he is still looking for you and the baby. I think we need to keep our eyes and ears open."

She couldn't agree more. Going after the ledger was a risky mission, but she'd been assigned to just as risky ones before. There had been a time in her life when risky missions were simply part of her job. Of course, she hadn't been traveling with a baby when she was in the Army. She was pretty sure she'd be better able to relax and focus on the task at hand once they'd passed Bella off to Ben. She would be safe and well cared for with him and Holly. And once the mission was over, she was sure they would work to find her parents who would love her forever.

Chapter 8

Harper raised her arms over her head in a slow stretch as Michael pulled into a motel parking lot shortly after the sun came up. It was small but cute, in a tiny town she hadn't caught the name of. They'd steadily climbed in elevation and were now somewhere in the mountains. There was snow on the ground and the temperature picked up from the vehicle sensor had dropped below freezing.

"We'll check in, have some breakfast, and get some rest. We are well on track to meet Ben at the rendezvous at dinnertime tomorrow. Wait here and I'll get us a couple of rooms."

She could see that Bosley needed to get out and stretch his legs, so she clipped the leash on his collar and let him out the back door. To say it was freezing was putting it mildly. Despite the fact that she had grown up in cold and snowy Minnesota, she had spent more than a decade in warm climates and wasn't used to the bracing cold anymore. She could see Princess's arms and legs moving slightly, so she knew she was awake. She would need to be changed and fed. Harper just hoped she'd hold off letting her know with loud tears until Michael had returned with the room key.

He was back to the car just as Bosley finished his business. She put him back in the SUV, then climbed back in as well.

"We're around back."

Michael had booked two rooms with a connecting door. Harper laid Princess on the bed and looked around the room. Modest but adequate. A queen-size bed, an adjoining bath without a tub but an adequate shower, and an old but functioning television. Michael brought in the diaper bag, and she got to work taking care of the baby's needs.

"I'm going to leave the connecting door open if that is okay with you," Michael said. "I'd hoped they'd have a suite like the one we had at the hotel, but no such luck."

"That's fine." She glanced at the old TV. "I slept in the car, so I was going to watch TV for a while after we'd eaten. I don't want to disturb you."

"I'm sure I'll be fine. I can pull the door mostly closed, leaving it open only a crack. I spotted a café down the way a bit. I can't see any way that anyone who might be looking for us would ever be able to find us here, so I think it will be fine for us to both go out rather than my bringing food back here."

"Sounds good to me. Just let me finish feeding Princess."

"I'll feed Bosley and take him out for a longer run while you do that."

After changing the baby, Harper warmed a bottle and snuggled up against the headboard to feed her. She would miss this quiet time together with the baby once they met up with Ben, but she knew that handing her off to him was the smartest thing to do. She'd heard Michael on the phone with Ben discussing the map and cryptic clues they'd found. From what she'd overheard, it seemed as if she and Michael were heading to New Mexico after they'd met with Ben. She'd never been to New Mexico before but had always wanted to. She'd seen photos of the miles and miles of high desert and found them to be both haunting and beautiful. Of course, she doubted, given the circumstances, they'd have time to do much if any sightseeing.

After the puppy and baby were fed, they drove back to the coffee shop, which was small but cozy and clean. The waitress had called out to them to sit anywhere, so Harper slid into a booth near a small Christmas tree with multi colored lights, setting the infant carrier on the seat next to her. They'd had to leave Bosley in the car and Harper felt bad about that, but Michael had done a good job of tiring him out, so she imagined he would sleep the entire time they were gone. Harper was glad that she could see the SUV through the window close to where they were

75

seated. She agreed with Michael that there was no way anyone could know where they were at this point, but it still made her feel better to keep an eye on things.

"Coffee?" the waitress asked.

"Please," both Michael and Harper replied at once.

"Special is sausage gravy over biscuits with two eggs for two ninety-nine, or we have a full menu."

"I'll have the special," Michael answered.

"I'll just have two eggs scrambled with sausage," Harper informed the woman.

"It looks like it is starting to snow again. Any word on the road north of here?" Michael asked as the waitress jotted down their order.

"It's clear for now, but it doesn't take much to close it. Best to keep your eye on the IDT website if you plan to travel north in the next twenty-four hours. Your order will be right up."

"Do you think we'll be okay?" Harper asked after she walked away.

Michael took out his phone and pulled up the app for the Idaho Department of Transportation. "I think so, but I don't think we should wait until dark to head out. After we eat, I'll grab a few hours of shut-eye and then we'll hit the road again. As soon as we get over the mountain, we'll look for a place to spend the night."

Harper took a long sip of her coffee. This had been the craziest driving trip she'd ever taken. She thought about the clues to the ledger that Isabella had left behind and realized, in all likelihood, that the truly insane part of it was most likely still ahead of them.

After breakfast, they returned to the SUV. She strapped the baby into the car seat and left the infant carrier on the seat next to her. Then she placed the diaper bag into it, while Michael greeted the excited puppy, who had been sleeping in the cargo area. It was only about a mile back to the motel, so it might have been okay to leave the sleeping baby in the carrier, but as far as Harper was concerned, it was better to be safe than sorry. The last thing she wanted was for the baby to become injured on her watch.

Michael slowed as they approached the motel. "Did you leave anything in the room?"

She stopped to think about it. "No. All we brought into the room were the baby and the diaper bag. Oh, and the dog bowls and food. But we packed everything up when we headed to the coffee shop. Why do you ask?"

Michael drove past the motel before pulling onto a side street. "Did you see that black sedan with California plates in front of the motel?"

"I saw a black sedan. I didn't notice the plates. Do you think someone followed us after all?"

He frowned. "Honestly, I doubt it, but I'm not willing to risk it. I think we should drive on."

"You've been driving all night," Harper protested. "Are you sure you're all right to go on?"

Michael nodded. "I'm okay. Let's get over the mountain and then take a look at the map. It may be time to adjust our route."

She turned and looked back toward the motel. "I really don't see how anyone could have followed us. Maybe the person in the dark sedan was just traveling the same route we are."

"Maybe. Call Ben and ask him to run the plates." Michael rattled off the license number he'd noted when they'd driven by.

She called Ben, who promised to run the plates right away and call them back.

"No one even knows I'm with you," Harper pointed out. "I think you're being overly cautious."

"I did pull into the motel where you hid that first night and I did send the cop I encountered on a fake disabled vehicle call. I didn't notice him take down my plate number, but he might have. Especially given the fact that I have Minnesota plates and he would eventually have found out that the woman driving the car left abandoned at the scene of the accident was originally from Minnesota, I should have known better and dumped the car. At the very least, I shouldn't have used my credit card. If the cop I encountered made the connection between us, it would have been easy enough for someone to follow the money trail. I used my credit card both times we filled up the tank and when I rented the motel room here, as well as the hotel room in Oregon."

She supposed what he was saying was true: using his credit card probably had not been the best idea. "So, what are we going to do now? We'll need money for food, fuel, and lodging, and I don't have any cash."

"I don't have a lot of cash on me either, but we have enough fuel to get over the mountain. We'll have to figure things out from there."

Michael waited for twenty minutes and then pulled out onto the highway. He drove back past the motel only to find the black sedan now parked in front of a room two doors down from the rooms they had rented. He turned around and headed out of town as quickly as the road conditions would allow. If the person in the black sedan believed they were planning to stay in the rooms they'd rented, hopefully they'd wait there for them to return, giving them a significant enough lead to lose them.

Ben returned her call shortly after they merged onto the open highway. Michael put it on speaker. "The plates you had me run belong to an official DEA vehicle. I can't say yet who the vehicle has been checked out to."

Michael pursed his lips. "I figured as much. I guess the CHP officer I encountered that first night must have run my plates. I'm afraid I've left a pretty easy trail to follow with my credit card purchases."

"Do you have cash?" Ben asked.

"Not enough."

"I'll bring cash with me to our rendezvous and we'll change out the car you are driving then. In the meantime, try to keep a low profile."

"It's snowing pretty hard and the guy following us doesn't have four-wheel drive," Harper informed him. "Chances are he'll be waiting for us to get back to the motel at least for a while."

"Let's hope so. Call me after you get over the mountain," Ben instructed.

Once they began to climb in altitude again, the trip became increasingly difficult. Not only was the snow coming down so hard that visibility was minimal, the snow was beginning to build up on the road. Thankfully, Michael's Range Rover had decent four-wheel drive and adequate tires. He assured her that as long as they took it easy, they should be fine.

"It's really coming down," she said nervously.

He slowed down just a bit. "Yeah. The road ahead narrows, and it is going to get dicey as we climb up the summit. I suppose the good news is that there is no way the guy in the sedan is going to be able to follow us, if that's what he has in mind."

She felt her pulse quicken. Having grown up in Minnesota, she was used to traveling in the snow, but she wasn't used to traveling in snow bordered by a mountain on one side and sheer drop-offs on the other. "I'm surprised they haven't closed the road."

"I noticed an IDT truck on the side of the road when we passed the point where they usually close it.

My guess is that we were the last vehicle to get through."

"Maybe we should have pulled over."

"If I didn't think we were being followed, I would have."

Her stomach knotted up as she looked out of the window at the sheer drop-off beside them. There was a guardrail, but she wasn't certain it would stop a heavy vehicle from plunging over the side should they lose traction. Michael was taking it slow and he had the vehicle in low four-wheel drive. He'd assured her they'd be fine, and she'd chosen to believe him. The snow was coming toward the windshield in such a way as to make her feel dizzy, so she turned her head and looked at the man beside her instead. Tall, broad-shouldered, and masculine, with dark hair and dark eyes. She knew he spent a good part of his life sitting at a desk manipulating a computer, but given his firm build, she suspected he also spent time either at the gym or involved in athletic pursuits.

"So, tell me more about Michael Maddox," she said to divert her attention from the road that she could no longer see. "Do you ski?"

"Of course."

"Water, snow, or both?"

"Both. I also kayak, mountain bike, and rock climb. What about you? Are you a fan of the outdoors?"

"You do remember that my fiancé and I were treasure hunters, right?"

"That's right. I remember you telling me that. Tell me about some of the places you've dived."

"The first trip I took with Eric after getting certified was to the Bahamas. He'd hired on as a diver for a salvage operator who'd already discovered and begun to salvage a wreck. I wasn't experienced enough to actually join in on the operation, but I helped out on the boat and was able to participate in recreational dives in the area. The three months we spent in the Bahamas sealed my love for the sea."

"I've never tried scuba diving, but I've always wanted to try it. I bet it is incredible."

She thought about the clear blue water, colorful fish, and warm sand beneath her feet. "It's really something. You definitely should learn. I'm sure there are classes in Minneapolis."

"I'm sure there are. Go on. Where did you go after the Bahamas?"

"Eric got a job as a dive master for a tour company. In the next eighteen months we traveled to Costa Rica, Australia, Belize, and Nicaragua. Eventually we signed on with a salvage operation in Australia. It was pretty exciting, but then Eric got wanderlust, so we moved on. After hopping around from continent to continent for a while, Eric met this guy in Puerto Rico who told him about a wreck he'd heard about off the coast of Cozumel. Eric had always wanted to go after his own treasure, so he quit the company we were working for at the time and we took off for Mexico."

"Did you find the wreck?" Michael asked.

She nodded. "We did. Unfortunately, it was that wreck that led to Eric's death."

Michael took his hand off the wheel for a moment and squeezed her hand. "I'm sorry."

She shrugged. "It's okay." She looked out the window. "I can't even see the road."

"Yeah, the lines are totally buried. We've reached the summit and will begin to drop in elevation. I might be able to make it off the mountain, but to tell you the truth, I am exhausted, and my eyes are beginning to blur. There was a sign a half mile back for a camp coming up. It looked like they had cabins. I think we should stop."

"They'd be seasonal cabins, wouldn't they? They'd be closed now," she pointed out.

"Still better than napping in the car. Keep an eye out for the turn off. If the cabins have fireplaces, we'll stop and rest up a bit. Not only am I about to fall asleep, but Princess must need to be changed and fed by now."

She realized that Michael was right. They all needed to take a break. "There," she said, pointing. "There is a road just beyond the sign advertising the cabins."

Michael pulled off the highway. The driveway hadn't been plowed, so he stopped shortly after pulling onto the private road to avoid getting stuck. "Wait here. I'll check it out. If it looks like an option, we'll hike in."

She turned to speak to the baby, who had begun to cry once Michael disappeared into the storm. "It's okay, Princess. I know you need to be changed and fed; it won't be long now."

Bosley stuck his head over the back seat from the cargo area. He began to whine as well. The time to take a break really had come and gone for everyone.

"There is a cabin not far from here," Michael came back and informed her. "We'll grab what we need and walk in. I'd try driving, but I'd hate to get stuck. You grab the baby and I'll grab the diaper bag and the bag of snacks I picked up at the last gas station we stopped at. The cabins are locked, so we'll need to break in, but I seem to remember that you are fairly proficient at doing just that."

"I can get us in."

The closest cabin was small. Really only a single room with a small bathroom in the rear, and the water was turned off. There was a fireplace, however, and dry wood stacked in a wood box on the covered porch. Michael scooted the sofa, which pulled out into a bed, over in front of the fireplace and then started a fire while Harper quickly changed the baby's diaper. She mixed up a bottle with some of the bottled water she had left, and Michael filled water he'd obtained from melting snow in the pan they'd found in a cupboard over the fire.

Michael gathered all the pillows and blankets in the cabin while Harper lay down on the pulled-out bed before the fire with the baby and the bottle. The puppy had taken care of his bathroom needs as they'd hiked up the road, so Michael saw to a meal for him and then he too snuggled under the covers with Harper and the baby.

"This is actually kind of cozy," she said.

"It is," Michael agreed.

"Should we be worried that the man following us will catch up with us?"

"He won't. I'm sure the road is closed now, and it won't be reopened until the snow has stopped and a plow has been through. By the time that happens, we'll be long gone." Michael adjusted a pillow behind his head as Bosley jumped up onto the sofa and snuggled in his lap. "We'll grab some sleep and then get back on the road. As I said, we are over the summit now, so everything from here to the valley is downhill. As long as we take it slow, we'll be fine."

Harper wanted to point out that they were a lot more likely to lose control of the vehicle on the downhill side of the mountain, but she didn't. "I'd say we should check in with Ben, but I suspect there is no service up here."

"There isn't," he confirmed. "I checked when we first arrived. Are you hungry? I have potato chips, beef jerky, and a couple of candy bars."

"I'm fine, but you go ahead."

He opened a bag of chips. "Are you warm enough?"

"Getting there. The fire is nice, but my feet are frozen after the hike from the road to the cabin."

"Let's take off our shoes and I'll put them near the fire. Socks too. They should be dry by the time we leave. Before we go, I'll look to see if there are any plastic bags in the cupboards. They aren't as effective as snow boots, but they'll help to protect your shoes in a pinch." Michael yawned. "I'm going to try to get some shut-eye. I've stacked enough wood near the fireplace to see us through the night. I intend to keep an eye on it, but if I fall asleep and you notice the fire has burned down, wake me. We'll want to keep it going or it will get awfully cold in here."

"Go ahead and grab some sleep," she said. "I'll keep an eye on the fire. I know this is a bit odd, but I'm kind of wound up."

Michael was stretched out next to her. The puppy curled up next to his stomach. Harper snuggled the baby close to her chest and promptly fell asleep. It wasn't until she woke up hours later and the cabin was freezing that she remembered her promise to watch the fire. Settling the baby on the sofa bed next to where she'd been lying, she climbed out and padded barefoot across the icy floor. Michael was snoring softly and she didn't want to wake him, so as quietly as she could, she stirred the coals, then layered several pieces of wood on the smoldering fire. She was about to climb back into the bed when she heard a scratching at the door. She looked toward the puppy, who was still fast asleep. She didn't think the noise sounded as if it had been made by a person, but she figured she should be sure. She tiptoed to the window at the front of the cabin and pulled back the curtain to find a face staring back at her.

Chapter 9

Harper screamed and jumped back.

"What is it?" Michael shot up in bed, disturbing both the puppy and the baby. The puppy started to bark and the baby started to cry.

"I'm sorry. It was just a raccoon. I heard a noise and peeked out the window and he was staring in at me. For a minute, I thought it was a person. I didn't mean to scream, but it startled me."

Michael started to laugh. The puppy continued to bark and the baby continued to cry. She looked out the window again, but it was gone.

Michael climbed out of the bed. "We should get back on the road." He crossed the room and looked out the window. "The snow has slowed considerably.

I'll take the puppy out if you want to see to Princess's needs."

She walked back to the bed and burrowed under the covers. "I guess I let the fire go out after all."

"It's okay. We should put it out all the way before we go. Let's do everything we need to get ready and then I'll put some snow on it."

It was another hour before they managed to change and feed the baby, walk and feed the puppy, and find plastic bags to make makeshift shoe covers. Harper hated to head out into the snow, but they had a rendezvous to keep with Ben, and she was anxious to get on to the rest of their journey, wherever the notes on the thumb drive might lead them.

The drive down from the summit went more smoothly than Harper had anticipated. The road was still bad, but the snow was no longer coming down at such a rate that it caused whiteout conditions. It took them the entire morning to get down low enough to find an open road, as well as functioning businesses.

"We're going to need gas," Michael said. "Check my phone to see if we have service."

"We do," she confirmed.

"See if you can locate the closest casino."

She raised a brow. "Casino? Are you looking to gamble?"

"No, but we need money and I have my checkbook with me. In my experience, casinos will cash a check if you have adequate ID. I figure that will get us by until we meet up with Ben, who can get us some cash for the rest of our journey, and the check I write today shouldn't be deposited for a day or two, so it won't give away our position until we are long gone."

"That's smart. It looks like there is a casino about sixty miles from here."

"Okay. We should have enough gas to make it sixty miles. Where do I need to turn?"

"There is a junction about fifteen miles north of here. We'll head east. I guess if we can cash a check, we can get a meal at the casino as well. I am starving."

"Me too. We can call Ben when we get there. We aren't going to make the rendezvous we set up. He may want to change the location. At the very least, we'll need to change the time. For all we know, he was slowed down by the storm as well."

By the time they reached the casino, she was desperate to use the ladies' room. The cabin hadn't had running water and she hadn't wanted to go outside in the cold, so she'd just held it in. She asked Michael to pull up near the front door and darted out, leaving him to see to the baby and the puppy. The casino was loud and bright despite the earliness of the day. She didn't understand why anyone would want to spend much time in any casino, but at that moment, beggars couldn't be choosers.

After she had taken care of nature's call, she went back out to the parking lot. Michael had the baby in one arm and the puppy's leash in the other hand.

"I'm desperate to eat, but I hate to leave the puppy in the car," she said.

"There is a lounge over near the gas pumps. It looks like animals are allowed inside. We'll make a bottle for Princess and then you can wait with her and the puppy while I go inside the casino to try to get some cash. I'll grab some food on the way back and bring it to the lounge."

"Sounds like a plan." She reached for the baby. "I'll get the diaper bag."

Michael took the puppy to the forested area beyond the parking lot to do his thing while Harper took the baby into the ladies' room to change her. Once Princess had on a fresh diaper and clean jammies, she headed back to the main lounge area, which featured several sofas, a grouping of tables and chairs, and a television that was tuned to the Weather Channel. There was a counter with a microwave on it, so she made Princess's bottle, then settled on to one of the sofas with her. The lounge was deserted, although it had appeared as if the casino was busy when she'd rushed through. She was just as happy to relax well away from the lights and noise.

"I was only able to cash a check for a hundred dollars, but that should be enough to fill up the tank and get us a bite to eat," Michael said. "Ben is going to bring us enough cash for the remainder of our trip."

"At least you were able to get that. Do they have anywhere with takeout in the casino?"

"There is a coffee shop that will box up our food. I brought a menu."

She looked at the options and settled on a club sandwich with fries, while he chose a hamburger. Michael hadn't brought any dog food into the lounge with them, so he purchased a couple of extra meat patties for the puppy. When everyone had eaten their fill, they went back out to the parking lot and climbed into the SUV.

"According to the IDT app, the road we traveled last night is still closed on the other side of the mountain. I don't see any way the guy from DEA will be able to follow us as long as we avoid using credit cards. Still, the car could be an issue, so Ben is going to trade us when we meet." Michael paused before he continued. "Going after the ledger will be risky. I want you to know I won't think any less of you if you decide to go to Moosehead with Ben. I'm sure he can find a place for you to hide out."

She looked at him. "Do I look weak and frail to you?"

"No," he admitted.

"Other than the fact that I screamed when I was startled by the raccoon staring in the window at me, do I seem timid or frightened?"

"No. I guess not."

"I was in the Army for ten years. Quite a few of them were spent in active combat. I don't mean to damage your manhood, but I would be willing to bet that I am better equipped to handle a mission to retrieve the ledger than you are."

Ouch. She could see him flinch. Maybe she had been too harsh, but she hated it when men assumed that because she was a woman, she was less competent than they were.

"Look, I'm sorry," she added. "I am very grateful for everything that you have done for Princess and me. I honestly don't know what we would have done without you. And I'm sure when it comes to figuring out the code used to create the map, your computer skills are going to be invaluable. I just want to assure you that you don't have to worry about me. I have been trained in counterintelligence and hand-to-hand combat and I can handle any type of gun there is. Well, I don't have a gun with me right now, but if I did, I could handle it. I want you to know that I can take care of myself."

"You're right. And I'm sorry if it sounded like I didn't think you were capable of handling things. Let's just blame my old-fashioned upbringing for my tendency to want to protect you. In truth, I wouldn't be surprised if you ended up protecting me."

She laughed. "Good to know. But the subject of guns reminds me, we should have at least one. Do you know how to use one?"

"No. In fact, if I had one, I'd probably shoot us both. But we'll talk to Ben about a gun for you. I'll do the computer thing and you can provide the muscle."

She smiled. "Deal." She turned around and looked at the sleeping baby. "It will be easier not having the baby to worry about."

"Ben and Holly will take good care of Princess and Bosley. I'm pretty sure the road we need to grab to head east is coming up. Pull a map up on my cell if there is service. I'd hate to miss it."

Harper picked up Michael's cell. She looked at the home page. "You have a missed call from Megan."

"My sister. I told her I'd call her about my travel plans for my parents' anniversary party. I suppose I should book my flight when we rendezvous with Ben."

"When is it?"

"Not for more than a week, but Meg has been worried I am going to flake out. Frankly, flaking out is exactly what I'd like to do, but she is really adamant that I show, and I guess I owe it to her. She does seem to be the glue that holds the family together. Or at least she tries to."

"I get wanting to avoid family gatherings. I've avoided plenty myself."

Michael turned toward her. "Why? Don't you get along with your mom and siblings?"

"I get along with them fine. It's just that it was hard to get home when I was in the Army. I was ambitious, so I spent a lot of time overseas. And then, when I decided that I'd had enough and hooked up with Eric, I was afraid that my family wouldn't approve of the choice I had made. Traveling around the world diving was fun, but it wasn't like I was making much of a contribution to humanity. I guess I figured my family would be disappointed in me."

"Did anyone ever say they were disappointed?"

"No," she admitted. "On some level, I suppose maybe I was the one who was disappointed in myself. I had a tough but meaningful life when I was in the military. After I got out and hooked up with Eric, I liked to tell myself that treasure hunting was important in its own way, but the reality was, I was really just messing around and wasting time while I tried to figure out what to do next. Four years of chasing windmills and I still don't know what I want to do with the rest of my life."

"You seem to me to be well equipped for whatever you decide. I'm sure you'll figure it out."

She certainly hoped so. "The turn is just up ahead. Less than half a mile."

After Michael made it, they settled into a conversation revolving around the pros and cons of classic rock and the country music that seemed to be so popular nowadays. Both agreed that given the choice, they'd take good, old-fashioned rock and roll any day of the week.

"Chocolate or vanilla?" Harper asked.

Michael raised a brow.

"Ice cream," she clarified.

"Strawberry."

She made a face. "Really? I've never acquired a taste for the stuff. It's just so fruity."

"Do you have something against fruit?" Michael asked.

"Not in its natural state. I'm not sure I am willing to take such a dangerous trip with a man who likes strawberry ice cream," she teased.

"I actually prefer frozen yogurt."

Harper laughed. "That's it. We are going to have to go our separate ways."

"Pizza or burgers?" Michael asked.

"Pizza. Yankees or Red Sox?"

"Yankees," Michael answered.

"Good choice. I guess you can continue to travel with me. At least for the time being. Although you do know that the best baseball team in either league is actually the Twins."

"Of course. Do you like baseball?"

She shrugged. "I used to watch with my dad, although his favorite was football. He took me to a couple of Vikings games before he died. I was the only daughter who loved football as much as he did, although I haven't had time to follow any sport much since I left home."

"Maybe if you are still in the area, we can catch a few Twins games this spring."

She smiled. "I'd like that."

"We should get to our rendezvous with Ben at around five. I figured we could wait to eat with him, but Princess will need to be fed and the puppy will need to stretch his legs before that. There is an app on my phone that lists rest stops. Check to see if there are any on this road."

Harper picked up the phone. She accessed the app and refreshed the phone's GPS when prompted to do so. The service in the area was spotty, so she had to wait for it to load. Once she confirmed the road they were on and the direction in which they were traveling, a list of rest stops appeared. She selected the one closest to their location. "There's one about thirty miles ahead on the right. It has bathrooms, a pet area, and vending machines. It looks like there is even an indoor lounge area, so I think it will meet our needs."

"Okay, we'll stop there. We'll call Ben and check in with him while we are stopped as well. I spoke to him while we were at the casino and he told me that the storm had slowed him down too, but he thought he'd be able to make up the time he lost today. Because we are going to get into town after dark, we discussed getting a motel for all of us and working together on the information on the disc drive. Ben is a smart guy and a good investigator. I'm sure his input will be invaluable."

"Yeah. Ben has good instincts. I'd welcome his input. Maybe once we get some cash and a different car, we will be able to lose our tail once and for all."

"We've probably already lost him, but I agree. I doubt anyone will be able to track us now that we know not to use my credit cards."

"Living off cash alone is going to require a lot of it. And if we are going to go after the ledger, I'm going to need some clothes," Harper said.

Michael shrugged. "I'm sure Ben can get us as much cash as we need. I guess you've heard that Holly came into quite a bit of money at around the time Ben met her. In addition to what she makes from her advice column, I think they're pretty well off. Once this is all over, I can pay him back."

"No, I'll pay him back," Harper corrected him. "I am the reason we are in the middle of this in the first place."

Michael didn't answer, but Harper suspected that the debate over who would foot the bill for this little adventure was not over by any means.

Chapter 10

Harper felt a sense of relief when Ben greeted her at the rendezvous point. She was going to miss Princess, but given the situation, she was happy not to have her health and welfare to worry about. Her instinct told her things were about to get hairy. Well, even hairier than they'd been up to now.

"You're looking good," Ben said after hugging her. "Tanned. I was so sorry to hear about Eric."

"Thanks. It has been hard, but he died doing what he loved. I guess that's all any of us can ask for. How are Holly and the kids?"

Ben caught her up while Michael unloaded the SUV they'd been traveling in. Ben had purchased a new vehicle in his assistant's name so that it couldn't be traced back to either Michael or Harper. They planned to drop off the vehicle Michael had been driving at a used car lot. Ben brought new burner phones for them to use, so they destroyed the old ones. He'd also brought a brand-new laptop that had never been connected to the internet, which they planned to use to read the disk. It seemed to Harper that Ben was taking unnecessary precautions, but given the fact that men working for government agencies were involved in whatever was going on, it was quite possible extra precautions were warranted.

Once everything was unloaded from Michael's old SUV, he went with Ben to drop it off with the man who had agreed to take it off their hands. While they were gone, Harper fed Princess and then clicked on the television. She needed to call her mother, but she didn't want to involve her if there was the slightest suspicion in her mind that her family phone had been tampered with. There was no way to know yet how far up the ladder Garcia's influence went. He was, after all, a rich and powerful man who seemed to have the ability to both make careers and end lives. She decided to wait to talk to Ben about how to handle things with her family when he got back. He knew her mother and sisters and would know how to deal with the situation.

******

Michael paused after returning with Ben. "She's fast asleep."

"I'm not surprised," Ben answered. "I'm sure these past couple of days have been hard on her. She is used to the counterterrorism stuff, but not so much the baby stuff."

Michael watched her as she instinctively tightened her arms around the infant who was sleeping next to her. The puppy had gotten up when they'd come in, and Michael knew that he would need to go out, but in the moment, he simply wanted to watch Harper sleep.

"That baby was lucky that Harper was the one to find her," Ben said after a few minutes.

Michael smiled. "I agree. She is really amazing. I'm grateful I was in a position to help her, but I'm certain that she would have found a way to get herself and the baby out of immediate danger with or without me."

Ben nodded. "I've no doubt about that. She really is one of the most capable people I have ever met. When Holly suggested I look her up when we realized the teenager I was looking for was last seen in San Diego, near where Harper was living at the time, I wasn't sure that bringing a woman into the investigation was a good idea. But boy, was I ever glad I decided to take the advice of my brilliant wife once I'd had a chance to meet the woman. I found Harper to be not only fearless but smart and intuitive as well. I honestly don't know if I would have found the girl before the human trafficker shipped her out without Harper's help. She seemed to know just what to do every step of the way, and she demonstrated a natural instinct that can't be learned."

"I guess that was why she was so valuable to the Army."

Ben nodded. "She was indeed. After working with her for less than a week, I could tell that she must have been a damn good soldier." He looked at Michael. "If the ledger really does exist, and the map and associated clues do lead to it, she'll find it."

"She asked about a gun," Michael informed his friend.

"I have one I can give her. She can use it, so I am going to suggest that you let her take the lead if push comes to shove."

"Yeah, she already made that pretty clear to me." Michael hooked the leash on Bosley's collar. "Harper told me a bit about her time in the military. Not a lot, just a glimpse. She seemed to have enjoyed the life. I'm kind of surprised she left."

Ben grabbed his jacket and followed Michael out the door. "Her best friend and teammate was shot and killed during a mission. They had been sent behind enemy lines to retrieve an asset who'd been captured. The enemy was waiting for them, and her team met with heavy fire. Her friend died, as did several other members of the team. It was tough on her. I think she felt like maybe their deaths were her fault. That maybe if she had done something sooner or better, they would have lived."

"Wow. That's awful."

Ben nodded. "It was. Her tour ended shortly after the incident and she spent the final months of her contract in San Diego, where she met Eric. She told me that after the death and destruction of war, his lighthearted approach to life was refreshing. He seemed to have the money to spend traveling the world, following one dive after another. She told me that she felt like she needed a change, so instead of reupping for another four years, she went with him. I guess she told you that he died while diving on a wreck."

Michael nodded. "She did tell me that. She didn't say why she decided to leave the Army, though. It seems like she's had a tough time all around."

"She has, but she is a survivor. I know that she is feeling somewhat lost since Eric's death, but I have no doubt she'll eventually land on her feet."

Michael turned back toward the room after Bosley had finished his business.

"I think the two of you will make a good team," Ben added. "You both have good instincts and you bring to the partnership slightly different skill sets. If anyone can find the ledger, I have no doubt it would be the two of you."

"I'll take good care of her," Michael promised.

"You do that, and let her take care of you as well."

After Michael entered the room he'd taken as his own, he went to look in on the woman who was still asleep in the next one. If he was honest with himself, after only a few days he already found himself falling halfway in love with her, but after learning the rest of what she'd been through and knowing the courage it must have taken to find a way to survive, he suspected he'd want to find a way to be with her even after this crazy mission of theirs was over.

Chapter 11

Harper turned around and looked out the rear window of the brand-new SUV that Ben had given them. "I actually thought I was going to cry when Ben drove away with Princess and Bosley."

Michael sighed. "Yeah, me too. I'm going to miss them."

"It is crazy how you can meet someone and be totally in love with them after only a few days."

Michael looked at Harper with a raised brow.

"The baby," Harper clarified. "I was talking about being in love with the baby. And the puppy. I mean, who wouldn't fall in love with that adorable little face?"

"Bosley is a cute pup and Princess is most definitely the cutest baby I have ever seen."

"Right! I used to think Holly was crazy for having all those kids; now I'm jealous that she gets to spend time with Princess while we track down the man who is most likely responsible for her mother's death." Harper's face reddened. "If I happen to get my hands on that guy, he is going to be a dead man."

"The plan is to find and retrieve the ledger and turn it over to the authorities," Michael reminded her. "Ben didn't mention murder as part of it."

"We'll see how it goes." Harper turned slightly so she was looking at Michael. "I didn't mean to fall asleep last night, and I certainly didn't plan to sleep clear through until morning. What did you and Ben manage to find out from the thumb drive?"

"There is a lot I still need to work out, but it appears that Salvador Garcia has a compound in the mountains of Southern New Mexico. Based on the information on the thumb drive, it appears as if it was from there that Isabella escaped."

"I wonder how she got all the way to California."

"I don't know. The timeline is sketchy, so I'm not sure how long she was on her own before she got hooked up with the DEA. I do suspect that she may have hidden the ledger near the compound rather than travel with it, yet not so close to it that it would be easily discovered. Keep in mind that she was pregnant at the time of her escape. Because I don't have a good handle on that timeline yet, I'm not sure how far along she was, but I am fairly certain she would have wanted to travel light. My suggestion is that we head toward New Mexico. We can work on the map in the evenings after we stop. I'm hoping to have more of the clues associated with the map translated by the time we get there."

"And how long do you think that will take?"

"Two or three days, depending on the weather. I looked at the forecast this morning before we started out, and unfortunately, there are storms all across the country for most of the upcoming week. I think we are going to need to deal with snow in the north and rain in the south."

Harper supposed that a road trip lasting two or three days wouldn't be all that bad. It would give her time to get to know Michael better and to try to decode the map. Without the baby and the puppy as buffers, she did worry that the situation might take on an intimacy she wasn't sure she was ready for. Of course, she had just met Michael. Still she couldn't quite get his soft brown eyes and crooked smile out of her mind. When she'd awaken in the middle of the night to find him pacing the floor with a fussy Princess, singing softly to her all the while, her icy heart had melted just enough to create a hole in her defenses.

"Pull up the weather app on my phone and see if the storm that was supposed to roll into southern Montana has arrived yet."

Harper picked up the phone and accessed the app. "It looks like it is currently snowing in Billings, with heavy snow predicted by late morning. It does look like the snow is supposed to taper off by midafternoon." Harper glanced at her driving companion. "I guess we can stop for lunch and wait out the worst of it and then continue south if the storm dissipates as predicted."

"Sounds like a good plan. Ben and I were up pretty late last night, so I was thinking we'd stop early today anyway."

"I got plenty of sleep and am happy to drive if you would like to take a nap."

Michael looked like he was going to argue but instead agreed that they'd trade off in an hour or so, and she could drive until they stopped for lunch.

"I've been thinking about the DEA vehicle we saw in Idaho. Do you think whoever was driving it wanted to do us harm?" Harper asked.

"I don't know. At this point, I don't think we can trust anyone. Ben has a friend in the FBI who he assured me we can trust. He is going to talk with him as soon as he has a chance to see if he might be able to get an insider's look at the players, who might be on Garcia's payroll, and who we might be safe trusting."

"I just hope Ben's connection actually is one of the good guys."

"Ben knows what's at stake. He'll be careful."

As agreed, Michael pulled over after an hour and Harper climbed into the driver's seat. Once she was underway, Michael promptly fell asleep. The drive was somewhat boring without him to talk to, and given some of the lusty thoughts she'd had after realizing that they were going to be alone for several days at least, she realized that allowing her mind to wander was not a good thing, so she turned the radio on low and hoped it wouldn't wake him. He must have been really out of it, she decided, because he didn't stir at all until she pulled into the parking lot of a strip mall.

Michael sat up and looked around. "Why are we stopping?"

"It's just past noon and we'd decided to stop for lunch."

Michael frowned. "I don't see a restaurant."

"Next door. I thought it might be better to park here."

Michael rubbed his eyes. "Why?"

She shrugged. "It was a tactical choice. Are you hungry?"

"Starving."

"Then let's go. The storm seems to have stalled. Maybe we can make more progress today than we thought."

The coffee shop was crowded, but they managed to find a booth near a window. Michael ordered a roast beef sandwich with a cup of vegetable beef soup, and she chose a grilled cheese with a cup of tomato soup. They were halfway through their meal when she noticed the car.

"Black sedan with California plates."

Michael frowned. "There is no way that guy followed us."

She watched as a man got out of his car and looked around the parking lot. There were at least two dozen cars in the lot, but he paused and looked in the window of every single one.

"Come on," Michael said, grabbing his jacket, tossing a couple of twenties on the table, and heading toward the bathrooms and the back door.

"It can't be the same guy," she said, following Michael out into the cold.

"Maybe not, but it looks like the same car."

She followed Michael as he crept around toward the front of the lot, being careful to stay low so the hedge growing against the building would hide them. Her view of the man dressed in casual clothes was filtered, but it was good enough to see that he was not the man who had killed Agent Beaverton. Still, she found herself wishing she hadn't left the gun Ben had given her locked in the glove box.

"They aren't here," the man was saying into his phone. "Yes, I'm sure. There are a couple of dozen cars in the lot but not a single Range Rover."

Her heart pounded as the man paused to listen to the person on the other end of the line. She prayed he wouldn't hear her breathing; it sounded loud to her ears.

The man continued to listen for a while longer, then spoke. "I looked inside every car in the lot and there wasn't a car seat in any of them. I can't explain why the GPS signal said they would be here, but they aren't."

She held her breath as he glanced in their direction. Again, she wished she had brought the gun. Of course, even if she'd had, she wasn't sure what she'd have done with it. There were a whole lot of innocent bystanders here.

"Yeah, I'll take a look inside. I need to use the head anyway. I'll call you back in a few minutes." He hung up and headed for the front door of the coffee shop.

Michael grabbed her hand and led her toward the other parking lot. Once they were loaded into the vehicle, he pulled out and headed back the way they had come so they didn't have to pass the restaurant.

"What GPS signal?" she asked.

"I don't know. This is a new car, Ben gave us new burner cells, and we have a computer that has never been connected to the internet. The old computer and phones were destroyed. It makes no sense."

She looked around frantically. There had to be something they were missing. "Your personal cell. We haven't used it to make calls, but we have used the apps."

"Of course." Michael pulled over. He got out of the car, put his cell phone under the tire of the car, got back in, and ran over it.

"Well, I guess that takes care of that," she said. "But now we don't have a map."

"The car has a navigation system. It isn't registered to either of us, so it shouldn't alert anyone if we use it. Look for a road we can take that will get us off this road and take us south."

She turned on the navigation system and pulled up the map. "If you take the next left and then the second left after that, you should run into Highway 89 South. If you follow that route, we will end up in Yellowstone National Park. The road through the park will be closed, but it wouldn't be a bad place to spend the night. There is a town there and it is definitely off the beaten path."

"Okay, we'll head there and regroup." Michael turned to her and smiled. "It seems your tactical move to park in the lot next to the restaurant paid off. I doubt this car will even be on the radar of the man in the DEA vehicle."

She shrugged. "It is what I was trained for." She looked at the navigation system. "I do think we should disable the GPS, though, just in case. We can buy paper maps to use, the way they did in the olden days."

Michael nodded. "I need to fuel up. I'll disable the system when we stop. Maybe we can find a travel plaza that sells old-fashioned maps. I wouldn't mind grabbing a snack considering we only managed to eat half our lunch."

"I saw a stand with maps in the last gas station we stopped at. I don't think everyone has navigation systems in their vehicles, and there are a lot of dead spaces out here, with no cell service."

"That's a good point. If we are going to stop early, we can work on decrypting the thumb drive some more. My gut tells me that the only way we can end this is if we can find what we need to locate the man behind it."

Chapter 12

The motel was located on the bank of a rushing river that provided a steady hum even with the windows closed. The lodging property didn't offer suites, so Michael got two rooms with a connecting door, much like other rooms they had shared before. The units were clean but somewhat shabby, although Harper supposed it really didn't matter; they were there to work, not to lounge around as if they were on an actual vacation.

"So, what did you and Ben figure out after I fell asleep last night?" she wondered.

Michael pulled out the laptop Ben had brought for him to use, set it on the small table by the window, and plugged it in. Once it booted up, he inserted the thumb drive, then accessed the file with the map. In addition to a topographical map that contained changes in elevation but no other defining attributes, there was a series of instructions that appeared to be written more as clues to a puzzle.

"As you can see, the topographical map alone doesn't tell us anything without other landscape markers. Ben called his friend, Special Agent Roy Griswold at the Federal Bureau of Investigation, and asked for his help in identifying the landscape."

"Did Ben explain everything that was happening?" she asked.

"No. As a start, Ben simply told his friend that he was working on a case, that the map was a clue, and that he needed help matching the map with the topography it showed. I have to say that I was pretty surprised when the agent didn't even question Ben's need to obtain the information. He just asked us to email him a copy of the map, which he ran through a software program that matches up topography indicated on a map with physical topography. Griswold came up with a location in the southern part of New Mexico. The problem is that the area shown on the map covers more than a hundred square miles. We are going to need to narrow it down if we have any hope at all of finding the ledger, assuming the map even leads to it."

"Which is where the clues provided in the puzzle must come in," she speculated. "I assume your plan is to travel to the general area and then look for the clues provided."

Michael nodded. "That's the plan. We'll need at least two days to get to our destination; maybe three days, depending on the weather. There are a couple of different routes we can take, so I thought we'd look at the weather report in the morning and select the one that is least likely to give us issues."

She sat back and looked at the map. "And once we get there, if we are successful in locating the ledger, then what?"

"Then we have a decision to make. I know Agent Beaverton told you to trust no one, but I think there is going to come a time when we'll need to bring in the big guns. Ben seems to think we can trust Griswold. He is leaving the decision to involve him to a greater extent up to us, but I trust Ben, so at this point I am inclined to give him the go ahead to talk to him again."

Harper paused to consider. "I get that we are going to need more help at some point. I'd like to wait until Ben gets home and Princess is safe with Holly. I guess he should be there tomorrow evening. Right now, I am inclined to tell Ben to wait to bring his friend in on more things until after we have the chance to look for the ledger. We both know that once any more of the feds get involved, they are going to want us to be uninvolved. We have come this far without them; personally, I'd like to see this mission through to completion."

Michael nodded. "That sounds fine to me. We'll call Ben tomorrow evening to check in with him." He logged out of the file that contained the map and logged in to the one with the information on bank accounts and contact names. "It seems like this file covers a lot of damaging information. I wonder what the ledger has that isn't already provided here."

She frowned. "Maybe the ledger is more of a calendar. I would think the number one thing that would be needed to actually track this man down is the knowledge of where he is going to be at some point in the future."

He sat back in his chair. "That makes sense. Perhaps the ledger has information relating to meetings that have been set up but have not yet taken place."

She tilted her head slightly. "Don't you think Garcia would change things up if that was the purpose of the ledger and he knew it was missing?"

"Perhaps. But there is an equally likely possibility that he wouldn't want to act in a manner that creates a sense of doubt in his own people, especially if he isn't sure the ledger has been compromised."

Harper leaned forward and rested her elbows on the table. "You could be correct about that. I'm sure Garcia wouldn't want his contacts to know that anything involving him has been compromised. It would demonstrate weakness on his part. I suppose it is likely that he is hoping to track down the ledger before he is forced to change the plans he has already made."

Michael logged off the computer and pushed it aside. "Let's grab something to eat. There were only a couple of restaurants open when we drove through earlier and I'm not sure what time they close."

"I noticed a restaurant with an attached bar when we came into town. Chances are it will be open later than some of the other eateries in the area." Harper sat down on the side of the bed and began pulling on her boots. "I really do need to find a place to buy something else to wear. I'm pretty sure these sweats are getting ripe."

"I noticed a mountain outfitter when we passed through. I don't know if they are still open, but we can check it out on our way to the restaurant."

Luckily for Harper, they were still open and had a fair selection of jeans, sweaters, blouses, and even socks and underwear. She picked out three pairs of jeans, two heavy sweaters, two sweatshirts, two blouses, and three T-shirts. Tossing one package each of socks and underwear on top of the pile, as well as something to sleep in, she headed to the footwear section in search of warm and waterproof boots. Michael grabbed a few items as well, although he already had several changes of clothing that he had brought with him. Once they felt they had what they needed, they headed toward the restaurant.

"Oh look, there is a table by the fireplace. Let's grab it," she suggested as she headed for it. "I wasn't expecting a lot, but this is really quaint. I love the log walls and the river rock around the fireplace. It feels very mountainy, and the Christmas decorations are really beautiful. I especially love the little ski village, in the window."

He picked up a menu. "The decorations are some of the best we've seen so far and the selection of food looks good as well. I think I am going to have a steak.

It's hard to know what our meals will look like once we hit the road again tomorrow."

"It does seem like we will probably be driving through some pretty barren country tomorrow, no matter which route we decide to take. We should find a store and stock up on water and healthy snacks for the road. A lot of these little touristy-type towns close down for the winter, so there might not be a lot of dining options available."

"I noticed the gas station near the motel had a minimart. We'll fill up and grab some snacks before we set off in the morning."

The waitress greeted them then, and Harper picked up the menu. She chose grilled salmon with rice and mixed veggies, while Michael ordered the sirloin with a baked potato and broccoli. They each ordered a cup of the clam chowder to start, which the waitress brought with a loaf of bread hot from the oven. In another situation, Harper might have ordered wine, but with the importance of the journey they had committed to, she thought she'd better stick with coffee.

"So, did you make your travel arrangements for your parents' anniversary party?" she asked after their soup had been served. Not that she was the sort to ask that sort of question under normal circumstances, but a family party seemed to represent a neutral topic appropriate for the time and place.

"Not yet. But I will."

Harper raised a brow.

"I will," he repeated firmly. "We've just been a little busy. I know that Megan is worried that I won't be able to get a flight if I don't plan ahead, especially with Christmas just a week after the party, but a single person traveling to a major airport can almost always find a seat somewhere."

"I suppose that's true. I traveled standby a lot of the time when I was in the Army. It was a pain, but I always ended up getting where I needed to be. I guess at this point the bigger problem is us completing this mission before the party rolls around."

"We have time." Michael took a sip of his coffee. "If not, I guess we can take a break from our search for the ledger so I can fly home for the party and then pick it up the following day."

"I would be willing to bet that your sister will want you to be home for more than a day. In fact, I'm surprised she didn't ask you to stay through Christmas."

"She did ask me to stay but I declined."

"You aren't the big family holiday sort of guy?"

"It's not that. Now that my parents have decided to downsize and have moved from New York to the Cape, there really isn't a home to go home to. Everyone has spread out and any semblance of a family home is gone. Meg lives in a tiny apartment in Boston, and as I've said, Macy lives in Alaska and Marley is in Italy. Even Matthew moved from New York to New Hampshire. In my mind, attending the party is a one-day obligation, and one day is exactly what I plan to commit to it."

Harper thought about her own family home. The huge farmhouse with eight bedrooms, five baths, and a large living area, had once been lived in by the members of a commune who had first settled on the property. After Denver bought them out, it was just her grandmother, grandfather, and mother in the huge house for a time, but then her mother met her father and they filled the bedrooms with five daughters. Harper couldn't imagine the family farmhouse no longer being in the family. Sure, she hadn't visited in fourteen years, but she knew that her room would be waiting for her, just like Hayden's room was waiting for her when she visited from Minneapolis.

Haven was the only daughter to actually still live in the house. Haley had converted the old barn on the grounds into a home that Harper had never seen but had heard was very nice, and Harlow lived in a small apartment above the bookstore she owned. Harper supposed that the house was somewhat large for just her mother, grandmother, and youngest sister, but in her wildest dreams it had never occurred to her that her mother might want to sell the place and downsize in the future.

"Do you miss it?" she asked. "The house you grew up in?"

"Sometimes," Michael admitted. "I guess what I really miss are the memories, both good and bad, I feel as if I left within the walls of the old place. When I moved out, it never occurred to me that my parents would sell it. I figured that I could go and live my life and it would be there waiting whenever I wanted to visit."

"Do you think you would have visited more often if your parents hadn't moved?"

Michael shook his head. "No. Not after what happened with Matthew and Julia. I love my brother, and I guess in some way I still love Julia. I want what is best for them, and from what my sisters have told me, they appear to be happy. But the fact that I wish them well doesn't mean I want a front-row view of their happy life together. A life that part of me still feels should have been mine."

Harper put her hand over his. "I'm sorry. It must have been such a brutal betrayal for you. But I'm sure that in time you will find someone who fills the void in your life Julia left behind."

Michael sighed. "Yeah. I know. I guess now that I've had a chance to gain some perspective, I can see that we weren't right for each other and most likely wouldn't have been happy even if we had married. I'm not even sure my feelings have as much to do with Julia's desertion as they do with Matthew's betrayal. He was my twin. My best friend. We'd shared everything in the past, but sharing Julia was not something I was prepared to do."

The conversation paused as the waitress brought the main course. Harper couldn't imagine how hard it must have been on Michael when the person he loved most betrayed him at the deepest level. She'd suffered loss in her life, and while Eric's death had left a huge hole in her life, she didn't have the pain of betrayal to deal with.

124

Chapter 13

Michael woke early the following morning. He could hear the shower running in the room next door, so Harper must have awakened early as well. The rooms didn't have coffee makers, but he'd spotted a coffeepot in the motel office, so he bundled up and headed in that direction. The desk clerk was watching the Weather Channel, so he paused to catch the latest update.

"Looks like we are going to have stormy weather for another week," the young man behind the counter said.

"Yeah." Michael poured coffee into the first of two paper cups he'd taken from the stack on the table. "It looks that way. We are heading south, so hopefully the snow will turn to rain at some point."

"I'm sure you'll hit rain eventually, but you're going to have to deal with snow for another day at least. The route through Denver is longer, but the roads are somewhat better during a heavy snow than the one through Salt Lake. You might want to call ahead about closures over the passes."

"I'll do that." Michael slipped a lid on the first of the two cups, then poured coffee in the second. "Do you know where we can grab some breakfast?"

"Marie's Diner is open during the off-season. Just hang a right after pulling out of the parking lot. The diner is about a half mile down on your left. Marie has a full menu, but I'd order the biscuits and gravy. They are the best you will find anywhere."

"Thanks for the tip. I'm also looking for road maps. Paper maps, in case we lose cell service."

"Toby's Gas Station on the way out of town has a good selection of maps. He'll be on the right after you leave the town limits. Best pick up some gas as well. Not a lot of stations open around here this time of the year. If you don't have chains, you might want to buy a set before you head out. A lot of folks with four-wheel drive vehicles don't think they need chains. A lot of them wind up getting stuck."

Michael nodded. "Thanks for the suggestion. I don't have chains, but there were a few points along this trip they would have been welcome. I guess it is a good idea to carry some just in case."

"Seems to me there are a lot of motorists who die in these parts every year because they head out unprepared for the worst. My motto is to prepare for the worst but hope for the best."

Michael thanked the clerk again and then left the office with his two cups of coffee. He hoped Harper was ready to go. Biscuits and gravy were sounding better and better the longer he was outdoors, where the predicted high temperature for the day was a whopping eleven degrees.

******

Harper could hear Michael moving around in the adjoining room. She hadn't slept well and was at the point where she'd give her left arm for a cup of coffee. She'd looked around, but there wasn't a coffeepot anywhere. After she dressed and dried her hair, she knocked on the door between them. She hoped Michael was up and that he was ready to hit the road. She was sure there was coffee to be found somewhere in this town.

"Oh good, you're ready." Michael handed her a cup of coffee after opening the door. "I found out where we can get breakfast, fuel, maps, and other supplies for the road."

Harper took a long sip of the really terrible coffee. "You are a god." She took another sip despite the taste. At least it had caffeine. "The sky is looking particularly ominous this morning. I hope we don't end up getting snowed in somewhere."

Michael frowned. "Yeah. It isn't the best day for traveling, but I don't want to waste a day. We have blankets in the car and I'm going to buy some tire chains. I figure we'll stock up on snacks and water as well. If we end up in another seasonal cabin, I think we'll be fine. Be sure to wear the heavy wool socks you bought last night. It's freezing outside."

Harper pulled on her heavy socks and lined boots. "I would think you would be used to the cold by now."

"I'm not sure this is the sort of cold you ever get used to."

"I don't remember Moosehead winters being terribly awful, but I did leave when I was eighteen, and I have been living in locations where a cold spell means the temps have dipped below sixty since then. I'm sure I'll need to reacclimate a bit. If I decide to stay, that is." Harper grabbed her new down jacket and fuzzy brown hat and mittens.

"Do you think you will stay in Moosehead? For a while at least?"

Harper stepped out onto the walkway and closed her door behind her. "For a while, yes. Definitely until Princess is settled with a family she can grow up with and have a good life. I know that would be what Isabella wanted for her. What she risked everything to ensure. It's what I want for her as well."

Michael took Harper's gloved hand in his own. "Yeah. Me too. Don't worry, we'll figure this out one way or another."

******

Breakfast was adequate, although Harper didn't think the biscuits and gravy were quite as good as the desk clerk had assured Michael they would be. They ordered an extra coffee each for the road and then headed toward the little convenience store and gas station where they stopped to buy maps, snacks, tire chains, and water. After Harper picked out both some healthy choices and some junk food for the road, she went to wait for Michael in the SUV, while he fueled up and paid for everything. If this road trip hadn't been so important, and if Princess's life hadn't been on the line, she might actually be enjoying herself. She'd never taken a long trip cross-country and she found the landscape to be gorgeous despite the snow.

"I've been thinking about the map," Harper said after they got underway.

"What about the map?" Michael asked.

"The clues that are provided with the topographical map are clearly encoded. Based on what we know of Isabella, she was just a teenager when she hooked up with a much older, dangerous man. While we can assume that she was street smart given the fact that she managed to escape the compound in New Mexico after traveling to the United States with Garcia, she most likely was not highly educated."

"Which means that she had help with the code," Michael responded. "Which also means that at least one person other than Isabella knows or knew of the location of the ledger."

Harper nodded. "Exactly. If it was Agent Beaverton who helped her and he didn't pass the information on to anyone else, the location may have died with him. If, however, it was someone else who helped her, or if Beaverton shared the information with someone before he knew about the mole, we should expect that we may not be the only ones looking for the ledger wherever it is most likely hidden."

Michael frowned. "I was hoping we wouldn't need to look over our shoulders for this entire trip."

"A smart soldier always looks over their shoulder."

Michael blew out a breath. "Okay, I guess that we will continue as planned but take extra precautions, especially when we get into New Mexico. I was actually thinking we ought to be extra careful once we crossed the border from Colorado anyway, because we really have no way of knowing if Garcia is still at his compound or if he knows that there may be someone other than him looking for the ledger."

"If Isabella took the ledger from the compound, it is likely that it is hidden within a few miles of it. The thought of having to get that close to the place where Princess's father might very well be hiding out doesn't thrill me, but I suppose there are a lot of assignments I have been less than thrilled with that worked out fine in the end."

He glanced at her. "I have to admit that I am having a hard time picturing you in a combat situation. It must have been intense."

Harper paused before she answered. She felt a tug in her chest at her memories. "They were intense, but somehow in the moment when you penetrate enemy lines and are staring in the eyes of the person who has been tasked with killing you, everything is just a bit too real to worry about being scared. It is almost like the primal part of your consciousness knows that fear has no place in the situation, so you do what you've been trained to do and don't worry about the rest. At least, that was the way it was for me. I'm sure different people experience intense situations like the type my team were assigned differently."

She turned around and grabbed a bag of potato chips out of the grocery sack on the seat. She opened the top and popped one into her mouth. She offered the bag to Michael, but he declined. They hadn't gotten much exercise since they'd been on the trip and she probably should have passed on the chips, but she was hungry. Okay, she wasn't exactly hungry, she was just a bit agitated by their discussion of her time in the Army, and wasn't being agitated much the same thing as being hungry?

"We just passed a sign for a rest stop," Michael said. "I think we'll take a short break. Maybe walk around a bit and stretch our legs."

"Sounds good. I could use a walk. Do you think we should call Ben? See how he is doing with Princess and Bosley?"

Michael pulled onto the off-ramp to the rest stop. "I'm sure Ben is doing fine with both of them. He has more experience with babies than both of us put together, and at last count, the Holiday family had six dogs. We'll call him this evening. I hate to bother him while he is driving if it isn't an absolute emergency."

"Yeah, you're right. I guess I am just getting anxious to wrap this up." She grabbed her jacket and slipped on her knit hat and gloves before getting out of the car. It was snowing lightly, but so far, the worst of the storm was still to the east of them.

"I'm anxious to have this finished as well, although I would be lying if I said I hated everything about the trip. Getting to know you has been one of the highlights of my life."

Harper smiled. "And I'm happy to have met you as well."

Michael took her hand and headed toward the heated building where the restrooms and vending machines were located. He popped a dollar into the coffee machine, then turned back to her. "If things go as planned, we should be able to find the ledger, turn it over to the feds, and get on with our lives by this time next week."

Harper found the thought of getting on with her life something to be both anticipated and dreaded. On one hand, she wanted Princess to be safe from anyone who would harm her, and she was anxious to figure out the next phase of her own life, but on the other, getting on with her life most likely meant that she'd never see Michael again. He did live in Minneapolis and she was heading to Moosehead, which wasn't all that far away, but it sounded as if he lived a full and busy life. "Do you visit Moosehead often?"

"Not really. I know I said I moved to Minnesota so that I could be closer to Ben, which is true, but I've been really busy lately and haven't had a lot of time to visit. I am planning on taking a break once we get home. I have my parents' anniversary party, but after that I might take Ben up on the ice fishing trip he owes me." He paused. "And of course I'll want to be available to help with whatever needs to be done until Princess is totally in the clear."

"Of course." Harper accepted the cup of coffee Michael handed her. "Any idea what we should do with the ledger if we find it?"

"I'm not sure yet, but a plan for the ledger is number one on my items to discuss with Ben."

******

Michael was exhausted by the time they reached the outskirts of Denver, so he pulled into the lot of a popular motel chain, only to be asked for ID upon checking in. They were supposed to be traveling incognito, and he wasn't inclined to show his ID, so he made up a story about his wallet having been stolen and offered his vehicle registration in lieu of

ID. The desk clerk seemed to buy his story and willingly filled out the paperwork using the name Cooper Callaway. After paying cash for the room, he drove around to the back of the establishment, where the room he'd requested was located.

"I had to lie about my wallet being stolen," Michael explained to Harper, and then told her the rest of the conversation with the clerk. "The problem is, I told him I was traveling alone so he wouldn't ask for ID from the other person in my party, so I was only able to book one room for the night. It has two beds, however."

Harper shrugged. "That's fine. That's something we should keep in mind for the future: that motel chains are likely to ask for ID even if you are paying cash."

Michael yawned as he opened the door. "I'm afraid that we might be looking at a string of dive motels for the rest of the trip. The 'I-lost-my-wallet' routine won't work with everyone."

Harper tossed the bag she was using for her clothes and personal items onto the bed closest to the bathroom. The room was decent and, unlike the place they'd stayed the night before, had a coffee maker. "I remember Ben saying that the vehicle he brought us was registered to his assistant. Any idea what his name is?"

"Cooper Callaway. He is actually more than an assistant. I think that Ben is grooming him to be a full partner in the PI firm. Ben has a lot on his plate, and I think he realizes that at some point he is going to need regular help."

Harper flipped open her bag and took out a heavy sweatshirt. "Have you met Cooper?"

Michael nodded. "I have. He goes by Coop. He is a nice guy. Smart as well. I think he will be a good partner for Ben."

"Is he young? Old? Close to Ben's age?"

Michael paused. "I guess he is around thirty. He has a degree in criminal justice and planned to apply to the FBI, but somewhere along the way he met Ben, who convinced him that freelancing provided a lot of opportunities that working for the government didn't."

"So he changed his life based on Ben's recommendation alone?"

"Well, maybe that wasn't the only reason," Michael admitted. "From things I've heard Coop say, it seems that at least part of his decision to alter his career path from the FBI to work with Ben had to do with a girl he met in Moosehead."

"Ah," she said. "That explains a lot. Do you know who the girl was?"

"He didn't mention a name that I can remember. I'm sure you will have the chance to meet him when you get home."

"I'm looking forward to it." Harper tossed the flannel sleeping pants and long-sleeved thermal T-shirt she had bought to sleep in onto the bed. "We should probably head out to grab some food before we settle in. I noticed a diner a few doors down. We can just walk."

"Sounds good. We'll call Ben after we get back to the room."

Chapter 14

Harper couldn't believe they had finally arrived in Southern New Mexico. The weather had not been their friend and the trip had taken a full day longer than they'd counted on. Along the way, they'd worked on the encrypted instructions that had been included with the map, and from what they could figure out, which wasn't a lot, they were looking for a location associated with the clue *where angels sing*, which, as best they could tell, should be somewhere in or near the Guadalupe Mountains. Unfortunately, from that cryptic message, they were left with an area that was way too large for them to simply start looking for something that fit; Harper knew they were going to need something more. And more was going to take time.

At least Princess was safe. Harper had talked to Ben, who had assured her that both the baby and the puppy had settled in just fine and would be welcome to remain at the Holiday farm until circumstances allowed them to find a more permanent home. Harper knew that Michael had spoken to his sister on the phone several times, and at some point he was going to have to head east for his parents' anniversary party, whether they were finished with what they had set out to do or not.

"Let's get checked into a motel and then we can take a look around town," Michael suggested. "I know we've only been able to decipher a quarter of the message, but it's possible that the 'where angels sing' part is something that is recognizable to people who live in the area."

"That's true. Maybe we can find a laundromat after we eat. I'd love to wash my clothes."

Michael looked at his watch. "It's early yet. We should be able to take care of everything this afternoon, leaving us all day tomorrow to try to find the ledger."

The ledger. The thought of finally going after the item that had already cost at least two people their lives left Harper feeling agitated and unsettled. She supposed it was all the waiting that was getting to her. She usually did much better in circumstances where immediate action was called for. Not that traveling from state to state to find the ledger hadn't brought a certain amount of danger, but in her mind, it had been more of a prequel to the main event. Although, as Harper had looked out the window at the passing scenery, she had decided that just because the ledger seemed to be the prize that everyone was after, it didn't mean that finding and obtaining it would guarantee an explosive climax. She had been involved in many missions during her time in the Army when an explosive climax resulting from enemy gunfire and plenty of it was a foregone conclusion. In this case, however, it was more likely that they'd find the ledger, hand it off, and be done with their part.

"There is a motel up ahead. It's nice-looking and it isn't a chain, so they may not care about ID," Harper said as she struggled with the idea that an easy ending would most likely leave her dissatisfied and unfulfilled.

Michael turned into the parking lot. "Okay. Let's check it out."

As predicted, the young desk clerk was happy to take cash and didn't seem to care about ID, because she didn't ask for it. They were given rooms near the outdoor pool, which was closed for the season. The rooms weren't connecting, but Harper didn't suppose it mattered. After they each checked out their own room, they agreed to take some time to get cleaned up and arranged to meet in the lobby in thirty minutes. Harper used her time to take a quick shower, change into the last of her clean clothes, and sort her laundry in the event that a laundromat was in their future. By the time she made it to the lobby, Michael was already waiting.

"The desk clerk told me that there is a small museum about a quarter mile down the road," Michael informed her. "She seemed to think the woman who volunteers there might be able to help us with our puzzle."

"That's great."

"She also said there is a really good Mexican restaurant just a few doors down from the museum, and a laundromat just across the street."

Harper opened the back door to the SUV and tossed the bag with her laundry inside. "It sounds like the perfect setup. Should we start with the museum?"

Michael nodded. "It is most likely to be the first to close. Do we need to stop for laundry soap along the way?"

"I'm sure the laundromat will have a machine selling detergent and dryer sheets."

Harper pointed out the sign for the museum, which was housed in a small adobe building. There was a fountain in front, which had been drained for the winter, and off to the side, she saw a garden that was probably lovely in the summer but was brown and dormant now.

A Hispanic woman greeted them at the door. "Welcome to the Guadalupe Mountains. My name is Maria. How can I help you today?"

Michael smiled at her. "My friend and I are on a kind of scavenger hunt. We are following clues that will eventually lead to a prize. One of the clues brought us to this area, where we were supposed to find a place associated with the clue 'where angels sing.' We hoped you might know of such a place."

The woman screwed up her face. "'Where angels sing?' It sounds like that clue might refer to a holy place of some sort. I'm new to this area myself, but I do know that there are two churches in town. I can give you a map."

"That would be helpful," Michael said.

Maria made a copy of a map she had laid out on the countertop where she worked. She circled two locations. "These are the town's two churches. They might already be closed for the day now, but if you need to get a look inside, there should be something on the doors to tell you who to call for information."

Michael picked up the map and glanced at it. "Thank you so much. Are these the only churches in the area?"

Maria nodded. "The only ones still open. There is a church up on the mountain that has long since closed. It won't be easy to get to in the winter."

"Would you mind pointing it out anyway?" Michael asked.

Maria took the map and drew a circle around a spot that looked to be in the middle of nowhere. "I can give you driving directions to the trailhead, but from there you would need to hike."

"How far of a hike is it?" Harper asked.

"A couple of miles, three at the most, but it is a couple of miles straight up the mountain."

She looked at Michael. "I guess we could do the hike tomorrow."

Michael folded the map and put it in his pocket. He stuffed a fistful of bills into the donation jar and thanked the woman.

"If you do decide to go up the mountain," Maria said as they started for the door, "bring plenty of water with you, and check the weather report ahead of time. The last place you'd want to be in a storm is up there on that peak."

They thanked Maria once again and then headed to the laundromat.

"I thought we'd put in a load and then go next door to grab a bite while it washes," Michael informed Harper.

"Sounds like a good plan. Did you bring clothes to wash as well?"

Michael nodded. "I stuffed them into a pillowcase and put it in the back. Hopefully, there will be enough free machines so that we can do all our laundry at the same time."

"What now?" she asked as they started their washers.

"Let's eat. I'm starving. We can try to come up with a plan after that. It seems that checking out the two churches in town might be our next move. I sort of doubt Isabella hid the ledger in the one at the top of the mountain."

"I agree. If she was already pregnant when she ran away, even if she wasn't all that far along, it doesn't seem as if she would have wanted to make a hike as steep as the woman in the museum made it sound."

"I was thinking the same thing. Of course, we haven't actually tried the hike. Maybe it isn't as steep as Maria made it sound. Or Isabella might have had help," he countered. "We already suspect that someone helped her with the encryption of the clues. We'll start with the closer churches and then take it from there. As for tonight, I'm thinking enchiladas. It has been a long time since I've had any really good enchiladas."

"I could go with enchiladas," Harper agreed. "And maybe even a margarita. If they make them, that is. I suppose it is cold for a frozen drink, but maybe a margarita on the rocks."

The restaurant they walked to was small and quaint and, like the museum, the building was made from adobe. The woman who greeted them at the door didn't seem to know a lot of English, but she had a sweet smile and was quick to bring them a basket of chips and a bowl of salsa as soon as they sat down. She handed them menus and then went into the back, where they could hear her talking to someone, probably asking them to come out to take their order, Harper imagined.

As they'd discussed, both ordered enchiladas with beans and rice. Michael had a beer and Harper asked for the margarita she'd mentioned.

"This salsa is hot." Harper waved her hand in front of her mouth after taking her first bite.

Michael dug a big scoop on a tortilla chip and took a bite. "I like hot."

"I do too, but this salsa should be labeled 'fire of hell.'" She took a sip of her drink, then ate a plain chip, and another. She could see that Michael was trying to appear unaffected, but he'd downed half his beer in what looked to be a single sip. Maybe that was the point, Harper thought: feed the visitors the hot stuff and sell twice as many drinks.

When the second woman brought their food, Harper asked for a glass of water. She graciously brought an entire pitcher to their table. She also brought over a cup of what she referred to as "mild and mellow salsa," which she encouraged them to try.

"Except for the fact that I probably have third-degree burns on the inside of my mouth from the peppers in that salsa, this food is really good. I wonder why the place is deserted. It is a little early for dinner, but not all that early."

Michael cut his enchilada. "This is a small town tucked out of the way. It appears to me that it must exist as a recreation hub for summertime visitors heading up the mountain. There probably aren't a lot of tourists here at this time of the year, and I would be willing to bet that the locals can't afford to eat out often during the off-season."

Harper took a bite of her rice. "I guess that makes sense. But in that case, I'm kind of surprised the place is even open in the winter."

Michael glanced toward the attached bar. "I suppose that even if the locals generally don't eat out, the bar might still attract the after work crowd. Once we finish up here, we'll put our laundry in a couple of dryers and then take a walk down the block. I'd like to get a feel for the lay of the land. Besides, this is the first time in a long time we don't have to worry about snow and a stroll down the street is even an option."

The sun was just beginning to set when Harper set off with Michael down the street. Unlike some of the festively decorated little towns they'd passed through along the way this town was dark and drab. Of course the mountains in the distance were really beautiful. She bet it was hot as Hades in the summer, but the spring months must be gorgeous. Not only would the weather be temperate but, from the photos they'd seen in the museum, the wildflowers were colorful and abundant.

"I think one of the churches that Maria circled as being currently open should be just down this street," Harper said. "She said it might be closed for the day, but although it is dark, it isn't really all that late. Maybe we should check it out."

"I'm game," Michael answered.

Like the museum, the church was made of adobe. There were three wooden steps leading to a heavy wooden door, which they found to be unlocked after trying the handle. Inside, the church was small and modest. There were two rows of wooden pews with eight pews in each row. Each pew looked as if it might be long enough to seat eight adults. The floor was covered with old wooden planks scratched up after years of use, and in the front was an altar made of stone. Atop the altar were several glass goblets and a Bible. To the side was a stand with candles that were probably meant to be lit for a small donation.

Harper took the four quarters she had left from the machines at the laundromat out of her pocket. She slipped them into the donation box, then lit a candle for Isabella, the brave young woman who had sacrificed herself so that her baby could live.

"If Isabella did hide the ledger in here, where would it have been?" Michael asked.

Harper looked around. There didn't seem to be many places to hide anything. There were stacks of hymnals at the end of each pew, which made her think of angels singing, but if Isabella had hidden the ledger among them, it would have been found long ago. There wasn't anything other than the pews and altar in the bare room. No doors to cabinets or hidden alcoves. The floor looked to be solid, but she supposed that one of the boards could have been lifted and the ledger tucked beneath. Short of ripping up boards, which she had no intention of doing, at least at this point, she wasn't sure how that theory could be explored.

"You know what strikes me about this little church?" Michael began.

"What?"

"The building and its contents are simple. Stark, even. But then, amid the simplicity, are those windows."

Harper looked up at the three stained-glass windows that lined one wall. "They are beautiful. It looks like they are on an east-facing wall. I bet they are magnificent in the morning, when the sun streams through them."

"The window in the center shows a choir of angels."

Harper studied the window. "If the window is a clue to the location of the ledger, maybe you have to be here when the sun is coming through to appreciate it."

"If the sun through the window points to the hiding spot, don't you think we'd need to know the specific date and time on which the sun would reveal the location?"

She nodded. "Sure. If this was a movie. But in reality, I suspect that the location indicated by the light streaming through the window would be a bit more general. Maybe the shadow creates a pattern or something. It's hard to say."

"I guess it might be worth our while to show up at sunrise to see what we find."

She nodded. "Yes. Let's do that. The worst-case scenario is that we don't find the ledger here. Then we'll follow through with our plan to check out the other two locations Maria circled."

Chapter 15

Harper decided that the problem with their idea to catch the sunrise was that they had to get up really early to do it. Not that she had a problem with early rising most of the time, but she'd tossed and turned for most of the night and was having a hard time getting going this morning. Michael had booked the room for two nights, so they didn't need to take time to gather their belongings and load the car. The plan they'd discussed the previous evening had consisted of heading to the church in time for the sunrise and then waiting in it until they either located the ledger or the sun stopped shining through the windows, at which point they'd have breakfast and then either call Ben about turning over the ledger, if they found it, or continued on to the next church on the list.

"It had occurred to me after we left last night that the church might be locked this morning," Michael said as he easily pushed open the door.

She yawned before saying, "I'm glad we didn't get up at the crack of dawn for nothing."

"Sunrise should be in about five minutes," he said. "Let's just stand back and wait for the show."

They sat down in one of the pews and waited for the sky to first light and then the sun to peek in through the first of the windows.

"Wow," she gasped at the colors that reflected off the walls. "It's just, wow." She stood up and began to walk around the church to view the spectacular event from several different angles. "I expected this to be pretty amazing, but I'd say it's spectacular."

"It is," said an old man who seemed to have appeared at the back of the church. "I come here almost every morning to witness what I have come to consider the highlight of my day."

"You live in town?" Michael asked the short, thin man with dark skin that looked like leather and thick hair as white as snow.

He nodded. "All my life. My name is Manuel."

"I'm Michael, and this is Harper."

She reached out to shake the man's hand. "It really is amazing to find these fabulous windows in such a modestly constructed church. I sense there must be a story behind the dichotomy."

Manuel nodded. "The windows initially were built for a church high up on the mountain. They were a gift from a man named Theodore Madison, a merchant who was passing through here when he fell in love with a local girl who stole his heart but refused to leave with him. Madison was willing to give up his life of privilege to marry his Anastasia, who, at the time, lived in the mining camp with her father. The merchant was very much in love, but he was used to finer things, so he spruced up the church where his true love wanted to exchange their vows and had stained-glass windows brought here from Boston. Once word got out about the church with the beautiful windows that was so close to heaven that, if you were quiet, you could hear the angels sing, people began to visit it from all over the country to see the windows and, they hoped, hear the choir of God."

"That's beautiful." Harper put a hand to her chest. "How did the story end? Did the merchant and his bride live happily ever after?"

"They did. They lived a long life and had many children and are buried in the little cemetery just outside town."

"So how did the windows end up in this church?" Michael asked.

"Eventually, folks stopped making the trip up the mountain to visit the church. The town priest at the time hated to see the windows decay as the building had, so he had the windows moved down the mountain and installed them here."

The sun had risen in the sky to the point where it no longer shone through the windows when the man had finished his tale. Harper didn't think the ledger was here. There was nowhere for Isabella to have hidden it. Still, she was glad they had been here in time for the sunrise. She wouldn't have wanted to miss the light show for anything in the world.

Harper and Michael wanted to find a place to have breakfast before they continued their search. It occurred to her that given the fact that Garcia's compound was so close to this little town, he might have people keeping an eye on the visitors who came and went from it. Harper didn't think they had done anything that would give away their hand so far, but they needed to tread lightly regardless.

"The breakfast burrito sounds good," Michael said when they located a tiny eatery that offered a bar with stools but no tables.

"You might want to ask for the salsa on the side after last night," she warned him. "I think I am going to try the poached eggs with chili verde."

Michael rang a bell that alerted the sole employee, who seemed to be both waitress and cook. He placed their order, paid for it, and then poured them each a cup of coffee from the pot that appeared to be self-serve. "So, do we tackle the other church in town or the one on the mountain?"

She paused, looking out the window. It was overcast, but any precipitation had been held at bay for the moment. "My gut tells me that the old church on the mountain is our best bet. It seems that it would be too risky to hide something in a church that is currently in use. No matter how well you hid it, it seems as if it would be only a matter of time until it was found."

"Maybe we would have better luck at finding the location on the map if we could figure out the rest of the clue."

"What does it say exactly again?"

"There are several numbers that Ben and I were not able to translate, followed by the words 'where angels sing,' and then several more letters and symbols that we also weren't able to decipher, followed by 'for all eternity.'"

"What makes the words you were able to translate different from the ones you weren't?"

"From what Ben and I could determine, there are four sets of clues, each with a different type of encryption. We suspect each set of clues contains three words because that was the pattern in the ones we were able to figure out, but there isn't any spacing, so we didn't know that for certain. The first clue is a set of numbers. I suspect it is some sort of substitution encryption, but if it is, it is not as easy as A equals one and B equals two."

"So there are perhaps three words followed by 'where angels sing.' After that are maybe three more words you haven't translated, and then 'for all eternity'?"

Michael nodded.

"It looks like it might rain today. Maybe instead of heading up the mountain, we should make a real effort to decode the rest of the message. I know you and Ben worked on it for several hours, but that isn't all that long in the grand scheme of things."

Michael nodded. "Okay. I'm up for that."

"The two sections you did manage to decode…what type of encryption was used? Was it supersecret government stuff?"

Michael frowned. "Actually, no. In fact, the two sections we figured out were coded using methods that one might find in a kids' book about coding and decoding messages."

Harper raised a brow. "Maybe that in itself is a clue. Maybe Isabella or whoever helped her was using a kids' book to encrypt the message."

Michael's eyes lit up. "Given the trouble we have had decoding it, that thought never occurred to us, but you may be right."

"So, the first set of symbols are numbers that you suspect correspond to words, although you have not yet found the key."

Michael nodded. "That is correct. The second set was a combination of shapes and numbers that I realized was a simple substitution code using high-frequency letters."

Harper made a face that conveyed the fact that she wasn't following what Michael meant.

"Let's say that you notice that part of the code is a heart. The heart seems to show up frequently, so if you're guessing that you're dealing with a substitution cypher, the heart would represent a high-frequency letter such as E. The idea is to randomly assign an E to every placeholder where there is a heart and then look for the next most frequently used symbol, which might be a figure eight on its side, and assign the letter A to it. Basically, you make a series of logical guesses until a pattern appears. It is not an exact science and it works better with longer messages, but Ben and I were able to use the trial-and-error method to figure out that the second set of characters most likely translates to 'where angels sing.'"

Harper paused when the woman brought their breakfast. When she had gone back to the kitchen, Harper jumped back in to their conversation. "Okay, so the first set of clues you have not yet been able to decode are numbers. The next set was presented as numbers and symbols that you believe translate to 'where angels sing.' What does the third set look like?"

"Dots and dashes. At first, we thought it might be Morse code, but it made no sense when translated using it."

"Maybe it is a binary code. The dots could be zeros and the dashes could be ones, or vice versa."

He raised a brow. "That's a possibility. We'll try it when we get back to the motel."

"And what about the last set of clues? The set you translated as 'for all eternity'? What cypher method did you use to decode that line?"

"The code was created using a simple grid. It took a while to fill it in with corresponding letters, but after quite a bit of trial and error, we thought we were finally able to figure it out."

"You know what we need?"

"A supercomputer?"

"What I suggested before: a kids' book of simple codes."

"I didn't see a bookstore in town."

"We can get a book online. I know we aren't supposed to log on to the internet using the new computer Ben gave us, but maybe we can borrow a computer from the desk clerk at the motel or use one of the burner cells."

"I have a better idea. I noticed a small library just as we drove into town. It might not have the book we need on the shelves, but I bet we can get the librarian to pull it up on her computer."

Harper was surprised at how well the small library was stocked considering the size of the town and the lack of local population. There was a book on cyphers for kids in the children's section, which they wanted to check out, only to be stopped at the desk because they didn't have a library card.

"Would it be possible for us to get a temporary card?" Harper asked.

"I'll need two pieces of ID, one of which must be a photo ID," the librarian responded.

Harper looked at Michael. She doubted that he would want to risk providing his ID just to borrow the book.

"How about I buy the book?" Michael suggested.

"This is a library, not a bookstore. We lend books; we do not sell them."

"We understand that you are hesitant to lend the book to someone who is just passing through town, but how about if you sell it to us and use the money to purchase new books?" Harper asked.

"A hundred dollars," the librarian said.

Harper gasped. "For a book that costs less than twenty dollars new and probably isn't even all that popular?"

The woman crossed her arms over her chest and didn't seem inclined to give an inch.

"Okay a hundred bucks." Michael counted out five twenties into her hand, and they left the library with their new treasure.

Chapter 16

Michael frowned as he considered the dots and dashes on the page in front of him. The idea that this could be a binary code made sense, but it would have taken more than someone with a children's book on codes to figure out what to substitute. "We have discussed the fact that Isabella, a teenager without much education, probably would have needed help to come up with even the low-level code described in this book."

"Yeah. So?" Harper turned to Michael.

"I can't help but wonder if we aren't making this a lot more complicated than it really is."

She sat down on the edge of Michael's bed. He was seated at the room's small desk, but there was only one chair. "Perhaps. But we have considered the fact that Isabella had help."

"That's true. I suppose she could even have found someone with a better education to help her. I suppose we may never know."

"All we can do at this point is follow our hunches and see where they lead. Where do we go now?"

"Let's start with the dots and dashes," Michael suggested. "We'll try switching them to ones and zeros and then I'll run them through a program that will convert the numbers to binary code and we'll see what we come up with."

"Do you have to log on to the internet to do that?"

Michael shook his head. "No. I have the necessary software loaded onto the computer."

It took a bit of work, but eventually he was able to determine that her hunch was correct, and the third set of clues translated into "their heavenly chorus."

"So now we have several words, followed by 'where angels sing their heavenly chorus for all eternity.'" Harper frowned. "Does that even help us?"

"Not really, unless the church is the clue. Maybe if we can translate the first section that seems to be a number sequence, we can figure it out."

Harper picked up the book. "I'll start looking for codes that use numbers to encrypt messages."

"I'm going to call Ben to tell him what we have. Now that we suspect that we are looking for simple cyphers, he might be able to help more. He does, after all, have access to the internet."

"Let me talk to him before you hang up. I think the time has come for someone to tell my mother something. She doesn't tend to worry about me, but it has been a long enough time since we've spoken that she must be looking for me to arrive in Moosehead any day."

Harper looked through the book while Michael spoke to Ben. She couldn't help but smile when she overheard him ask about Princess. Like her, the idea of children probably hadn't entered his mind yet, but also like her, the tiny baby with the huge brown eyes and thick black hair had wormed her way into his heart.

She wondered what would become of the baby. Would she be allowed to grow up in a normal family, living a normal life, or would the circumstances of her birth haunt her until her dying day?

"Hey, Ben," Harper said when Michael handed her the phone. "How is the baby?"

"She's great. The other kids adore her, and she seems to like it when they talk to her. Holly swears that she smiled last night, but I reminded her that babies that young can't really smile."

"I bet she did smile. She's a very smart baby."

Ben chuckled. "Yes, she is."

"And how is the puppy?"

"He is in doggy heaven between the kids and the other dogs on the farm. Joe and Reggie absolutely adore him. We have six dogs, but the last time we had a puppy must have been when they were babies."

Harper smiled. "I'm glad everyone is doing well. I miss them. Which, for me, I know, is odd."

"It's not odd at all. I want you to know that I will take good care of both of them until we can figure everything out and are able to discuss permanent solutions."

"I know. And I appreciate it. Listen, the real reason I wanted to talk to you is because I think we are at the point where my mom is going to start expecting me. I'm sure by now she has been texting and leaving voice mails on the cell phone I no longer have. I'm afraid that she will end up calling in the National Guard if we don't tell her something."

"I agree. I don't know if Garcia's goons have made the connection between you and the Moosehead Hathaways, but I don't think we should risk having you call your house. I'll talk to her to let her know what is going on. If she is really worried, I'll arrange a secure call between the two of you."

"Thanks, Ben. After my being in the Army for a decade, I think my mom has learned not to worry about me as much as she might about my sisters, but given the fact that I have been totally off the radar, I suspect she might be starting to become concerned."

"It sounds like you might be close to finding the ledger. Or at least decoding the message. If things go smoothly, you could be home in a few days."

"Have you figured out what we should do with the ledger if we do find it?" she asked.

"Michael and I discussed bringing in Roy Griswold of the FBI. He's a good guy who has helped me out many times in the past. I think we can trust him to complete the mission when we have the ledger."

"Okay, but he doesn't need to know about Princess or where she is, does he? We can share the part about the ledger and the notes Isabella left on the thumb drive, but I don't want to mention the baby until we arc a hundred percent certain that the danger has passed."

"Agreed. Michael wants me to wait one more day to contact him, which I have agreed to do. I think it is important that the two of you watch your back. Garcia's compound is not far from the town where you are staying. You have to assume that he might very well have spies everywhere. Be careful who you talk to and what you say."

"Don't worry, we'll be careful. I guess we'll talk to you again tomorrow."

After she hung up with Ben, Harper turned to Michael. "Problem?" she asked when she saw him frowning at the computer.

"No. I'm just trying to figure out this number sequence. I really do think we might be dealing with a substitution cypher of some sort, but I've tried several combinations, and so far, the letters I come up with don't seem to translate into words."

Harper got up and crossed the room. She pulled aside the curtain and looked out the window. As they had expected, it had started to rain. And not a nice, gentle rain but a downpour. It was a good idea, it seemed, that they had decided to work on the code in the motel today and put off the trip up the mountain a day. "Maybe it isn't a substitution cypher after all. Maybe it is something else."

"I suppose the numbers could be associated with an algorithm that could lead us to a location. Without the key, though, it will be close to impossible to figure out which algorithm to use."

Harper turned away from the window. "Assuming that Isabella left the clues and the map on the thumb drive with the intention of communicating this information on the ledger to someone else, who do you think it was? The file that had the video of Agent Beaverton stating that a mole had been discovered and he planned to move Isabella had been added to the thumb drive just prior to when they took to the road. Do we believe the other files were added before that and, if so, how long before they fled?"

"All good questions. I'm sure it would help us to figure out what the clues might mean if we knew who the intended audience was."

Harper sat back down on the corner of the bed. "We suspect that Isabella escaped Garcia's compound with the ledger. She most likely realized having it would give her leverage when it came time to work out a deal with US officials. We know that she managed to get hooked up with the DEA at some point. We suspect, given the fact that the ledger was not on her when she died and the map she left behind seems to lead to the ledger, that she hid it somewhere shortly after escaping rather than bringing it with her. It seems that Agent Beaverton was assigned to stay with Isabella until her baby was born. Furthermore, from the video on the thumb drive and the fact that she was still with him when she died, it appears she trusted him to keep her and the baby safe."

Michael nodded. "That all sounds right. Are you heading somewhere with this?"

"I'm just trying to work through the sequence of events in the hope of stumbling across the recipient Isabella had in mind when the map and the clues were added to the thumb drive. We can assume that Isabella didn't need the map or the clues to find her way back to the ledger. We can furthermore assume that if she wanted Beaverton to know where the ledger was, she could have just told him. The only reason I can come up with for why anyone would have taken the time to come up with this elaborate puzzle is because Isabella was trying to reveal the location of the ledger with a specific person in mind she knew would understand what the clues meant and how to decrypt them."

Michael leaned back in his chair. "Okay, I'm following you now. The question is, who was that person?"

"And did she send that person the map and clues in addition to adding the material to the thumb drive? And if she did send the map and clues to someone, can we trust them? I would have to assume she did."

Michael got up from the desk, crossed the room, and looked out the window. "Why use encryption anyway? If she wanted someone to know where the ledger was, why not call or email them?"

"Maybe she had a connection on the inside. Maybe that was how she escaped. If one of Garcia's goons helped her, maybe she arranged to leave clues to the location of the ledger for this person to find before she ever even hid the darn thing."

"Walk me through it."

Harper got up and began to pace around the room. Pacing always helped her to think. "Okay, so, Isabella, an attractive young woman, is somehow attached to a man who has both wealth and power. She finds out that she is pregnant, and her love for her child demands that she try to find a way to get both herself and her baby away from this cruel and dangerous man. The father of her child brings her to the United States, and at some point, she sees her chance to escape. This would probably be the point at which she established a relationship with someone on the inside. Someone in a position to help her escape. I'm not sure exactly how the ledger fits into things. As we've speculated, it could have been taken to use as a bargaining chip with US officials, but it could have been taken for some other reason altogether. Let's suppose that Isabella arranges with the person who is helping her to escape to hide the ledger and then to leave a map and clues to its location. Perhaps the reason the man on the inside helped Isabella at all was so he could get his hands on the ledger. It is hard to say right now, but if Isabella did arrange to hide the ledger and to leave a map for someone to find it at some future time, we can assume that the codes she chose to use were ones she believed that person would understand."

Michael turned away from the window. "I guess that makes sense. Isabella wouldn't have wanted to leave a note that simply said the ledger was hidden behind the statue in the church. She would have known that someone other than the intended recipient might find the clue before he did. In that case, an encrypted message makes sense."

"I think the best we can do now is try to follow the clues and not worry about the intended recipient of the coded message. I'm not sure we can figure out who that is yet, and if we get hung up on it, we'll lose a lot of precious time chasing something we may never know."

Michael sat down on the corner of the bed beside her. "Agreed. I could use a break. Do you want to try to find some coffee?"

Harper shrugged. "I wouldn't mind a cup, although we are likely to get soaking wet in the process."

"A little rain never hurt anyone."

Chapter 17

Harper woke to find herself fully dressed and in Michael's arms on top of his bed. How had she gotten here? She remembered going with him to find coffee and settling on tequila instead. She remembered coming back to the room to work on the cypher only to decide that it required a key they did not have. She remembered agreeing to set the frustrating puzzle aside until they had a chance to visit the church on the mountain the following day, which was where they hoped to find the ledger, or at least a key to the first clue, which they hoped would provide the information they'd need to find it. She remembered the conversation drifting toward issues of a personal nature. She remembered them talking again about her heartbreak when Eric died and Michael's pain when the woman he loved chose to spend her life with his twin brother.

She remembered stretching out on the bed, listening to the rain, and telling him about her time in the Army, including the horrors she'd experienced and the victories her team had celebrated. Then he had shared bits and pieces of his life in New York, and his decision to use his hacking ability for good rather than evil after Ben had gotten hold of him. She remembered laughing and crying. She remembered falling in love.

Michael's arms tightened around her as she moved away from him. He was snoring softly, so she knew he was still asleep. She scooted slowly toward the bottom of the bed, untangling herself from his arms as she went. When she was finally free, she headed into the damp morning and returned to her own room, where she had a good cry in the shower. She knew that the sound of the water hitting the tile flooring would drown out her sobs, but what she didn't know was why she was crying in the first place. Was she happy? Sad? Had their talk made her grieve for the future she'd planned with Eric but would never have? Or had their words healed her wounds and created a longing for the future? Had her night with Michael opened new doors, or had it only reminded her of the doors that had slammed shut forever?

Harper was left with more questions than answers. She was dazed and confused, and the only thing she knew for certain was that she needed to pull herself together before she joined Michael for the trek up the mountain.

******

He woke to find his arms empty. Had he dreamed the previous night? His head pounded and he was fully clothed, so he didn't think he'd dreamed up the tequila at least. Sitting up slowly, he looked around. He was alone in his bed, so, he figured, if he actually had slept with Harper in his arms, she must have wakened at some point and returned to her own room. Michael groaned as he ran his hand over his face. What had he been thinking? Harper had only recently lost her fiancé to a terrible accident, and here he was, whispering his most secret dreams into her ear. He slipped his legs over the side of the bed. When his feet came into contact with the sweatshirt she had worn and discarded, he groaned again. He remembered sharing things with her that he never had with anyone else. He remembered being weak and vulnerable, wanting to find comfort in her embrace, but he also remembered her words of encouragement, which had made him feel strong. He remembered their laughter and tears. He remembered falling in love.

Standing up, he grabbed some clean clothes and headed for the shower. He could hear the water running in the adjoining room and smiled. He had known he was developing feelings for this woman fate had thrust into his path for some time. He also suspected if he moved too quickly, those feelings were likely to lead to the same heartache he had experienced with Julia.

He hoped they'd find the ledger today. He hoped they'd complete the mission and go their separate ways. Not only, he reasoned, did he have a family party to get to, but he knew that if he spent any more time with this dark-haired beauty, he'd never have the strength to leave her at all.

******

When he knocked on her door, she opened it with a smile that she hoped masked the turmoil she felt. They'd only talked. Nothing had happened. She knew it was crazy to believe that she was in love with a man she'd yet to kiss. Love took time. It was something that started as a spark, then grew and evolved as lives were shared. She knew that love couldn't happen in an instant. That wasn't the way it worked.

"Are you ready to head out?" Michael asked.

She nodded. "Should we bring our things or are we going to keep the rooms for another night?"

"Bring them. If we find the ledger, things might happen quickly. I'm sure we'll want to head out right away. If we don't, but find reason to stay for another day, we can always check back in. The place is deserted, so I'm not worried about them not having vacancies."

Harper nodded. "Okay. Come on in while I grab the stuff I left in the bathroom."

"I'll just wait in the car. Get it warmed up."

"Okay. Have you seen my blue sweatshirt?"

"It was in my room. I packed it with my things. I'll get it to you later."

Harper tried to smile, but their conversation felt stiff and awkward. She hated that the easy relationship she'd shared with him seemed to have evaporated during their evening of sharing and getting to know each other. She knew Michael was still in love with his brother's wife. It was crazy of her to think that he would ever want more with her than they had now.

"It looks like the rain has stopped at least," she said as she slid into the front seat after putting her belongings in the back.

"I checked the weather forecast and it looks like it is supposed to be dry today. The dirt trail up to the church is likely to be muddy, though, so it might be a good idea to change into your heavy boots before we set out. Are you hungry? I thought we'd stop to grab a bite before we start up the mountain."

She put her hand on her stomach. "I'm not sure my stomach is ready for food quite yet. But coffee would be lovely."

Michael nodded. "I need to fill up the SUV's tank, so we can grab coffee from the convenience store. There are plenty of snacks in the back if we get hungry before we can get back into town for lunch."

She yawned and stretched her arms over her head. "I would love to get this wrapped up today. It seems like we have been on the road forever."

"I spoke to Ben. He knows we are hoping to find the ledger today and is ready to take over once we do. He has spoken to his friend from the FBI, and while he didn't fill him in on all the details, he did tell him that something might be going down and he may be called on for help within a minute's notice."

"And Princess?"

"He swore to me that he never mentioned the existence of the baby to his friend or anyone else. Other than Garcia's men, Loughlin and some other CHP, and the DEA, no one even knows the baby exists. He had the information on the thumb drive saved to his computer. He went through it and eliminated all references to the baby but plans to give the rest—the financial information and contact names and addresses—to the feds as soon as we are clear of this."

Harper looked out the window as Michael pulled into the filling station. "What will happen to her? To Princess? Will Ben and Holly keep her?"

Michael shrugged. "I don't know yet, but I do know that Ben cares about that baby almost as much as we do. He won't let anything bad happen to her."

He was right. She knew that Ben would do whatever it took to ensure that Princess had a wonderful life.

Michael pulled up to the pump and she went inside to buy the coffee while he filled the tank. Other than the clerk, who seemed totally uninterested in her, there was only one other person in the little store. Initially, she wasn't concerned about his presence, but suddenly, there was something about the way he looked at her that caused goose bumps up and down her arms. Maybe this adventure was just getting to her. Maybe she saw evil intent in every glance and encounter because the events of the past several days had trained her mind to see danger around every corner. Or maybe the guy was one of Garcia's men. She couldn't be sure, so it was better to be safe. She paid for the coffee, then went out to where Michael was just finishing up.

"There is a guy inside who seemed suspicious to me. I think we should watch our backs, make sure we aren't followed."

Michael looked toward the store. "Suspicious how?"

She shrugged. "I don't know. He just gave me the creeps. It might be nothing, but I think we should go. Right away."

"I agree. If we suspect we are being followed, we can make an additional stop to be sure."

He pulled onto the highway. She watched the rearview mirror the entire time. So far, no one seemed to be following them, so she began to relax. "Is the trailhead off this road?"

"No. According to the map, there should be a forest service road about two miles from town. It is a narrow dirt road, but with the four-wheel drive we have, we should be fine. Maria at the museum said to follow the dirt road until we came to a gate. That would be the point where we would need to park and start hiking."

She looked toward the overcast sky. "I hope the rain holds off."

"I think it is supposed to be dry until this evening." He turned his head slightly. "How are you feeling today?"

She put her hand to her head. "I'll live. I may never drink tequila again, but I'll live. How about you?"

"Same."

"I don't know what we were thinking. We knew we had this trip up the mountain today. Why on earth did we think it was a good idea to buy a bottle of the local stuff and toast our partnership on this journey?"

Michael adjusted the rearview mirror. "We've both been under a lot of stress and I guess we were beginning to feel the effects. A single toast would have been fine if we'd stopped there, instead of finding a half dozen other things to toast after that."

He had a point, she realized. It wasn't the first toast that had done them in, it was all the ones that followed. Still, she wasn't sure she would undo it even if she could. While the tequila might have been a bad idea, it had helped them to relax and to get to know each other in a way they might not have otherwise. She knew she'd always treasure the memory of Michael sharing the details of his summers in the Hamptons, and the painful event that had caused him to retreat into himself and trade outdoor adventures for summers in front of a computer. She supposed those long days at the computer had helped to make him the superhacker he was today, but her heart still bled for the teenager whose younger sister had drowned and whose parents had pushed away their remaining children for a time as they dealt with their grief.

"So, when do you need to go east for your parents' party?" she asked.

"If we wrap this up today, I plan to go directly back to Minnesota. I figure I can catch a plane from the MSP Airport, and you can take the SUV and drive to Moosehead."

She frowned. "I see. I thought we had more time."

"I thought so too, but my sister wants me to show up a few days early." Michael smiled, although it looked forced to her eyes. "You know how little sisters can be. Pushy and bossy."

She did know how that could be, but she had a feeling there was more going on than that. She decided to let it go. "Maddie. The sister who drowned. Was she the youngest?"

Michael nodded. "Maddie was just four when it happened. Marley was seven, Megan was ten, Macy was thirteen, and Matthew and I were fifteen."

"I'm sorry. I'm sure her death was hard on your whole family. I may have already said as much last night, but there seem to be quite a few holes in my memory today."

Michael chuckled. "Don't worry. Things will begin to come back to you once the tequila works its way out of your system."

While Harper was the sort to want to keep in control of her faculties at all times, she had a feeling that memories of the night before might not be her friend.

Chapter 18

Michael pulled the vehicle to the side of the road when they came to the gate Maria had told them about. So far it didn't appear as if they had been followed, which allowed him to relax just a bit. He recognized the importance of completing things today if he wanted to maintain his sanity *and* give Harper the space she needed to heal from the loss of her fiancé, so all his energies had to stay focused on finding the ledger.

"It looks like we just take this trail to the top." He looked up to where it crisscrossed up the mountain. A structure, he assumed the church, could be seen at the top.

"Wow. That really is steep." Harper took a step forward. "I guess we should get started."

"After you." Michael gestured for her to go first.

"I have to wonder why Isabella would hide the ledger all the way up on the top of a mountain, if that turns out to be where it is," Harper mused. "I don't know how far she was in her pregnancy when she ran away, but even if she was only a few months along, I would think she would have chosen a hiding place with easier access."

Michael could already feel his heart pounding in his chest. He suspected that Harper was going to leave him in the dust by the time they got to the top. She'd spent the past fourteen years engaged in active pursuits both in the Army and as a scuba diver, while he'd basically spent his time sitting at a computer. Sure, he went to the gym when he had time, which wasn't often, and he participated in several sports. But even if he'd been to the gym every day, he knew that the sort of workout he got there could in no way be compared to the one she got from everyday life. "We've speculated Isabella had help. Maybe whoever helped her brought the ledger up to the church for her."

"Maybe." Harper paused. "Would you look at that view?"

Michael paused and gazed out over the desert. It felt as if you could see forever. "It really is something."

"I like that we can see the parking area. I still think it is a good idea to keep an eye on the cars."

Michael nodded, then looked up to the trail ahead of them and groaned. He had a feeling the hike to the top was going to be even harder than he had imagined.

******

She found that she was enjoying the hike. It had been a while since she'd had the opportunity to test her body in such a beautiful location. She was a bit worried about Michael and the deep purple color of his face. Perhaps she should slow down a bit. It had been a while since she'd had any challenging physical tasks to complete, but even after Eric died and she had stopped diving, she'd kept herself in shape by running, swimming, and cycling.

"It's not much farther," she called back to him. Not that he didn't look totally fit and gorgeous, but she suspected that he wouldn't have lasted a week in the Army.

When they reached the top, she just stood in awe. "Wow. This is so… I have no words."

"It's beautiful. I love the way you can see both the desert and the mountains. It really is magical."

Harper looked toward the ruins they had hiked up to find. "I wonder what we're looking for."

Michael shrugged. "I guess a hiding place large enough to contain the ledger, or perhaps a clue that will help us solve the first part of the puzzle Isabella left."

She took several steps toward the crumbling stone structure. The walls were mostly intact, but the ceiling had fallen in several places. They'd need to take it slow and be extremely careful lest they themselves cause a cave-in. "Can you imagine hiking all the way up here to attend services? It must have been a bit like worshiping in heaven itself."

"I can't imagine hiking all the way up here for any reason. At least not on a regular basis."

"I think the mining camp is located in this area. It could be that the hike from the camp wasn't all that bad. Oh, look." She pointed toward a wall that had been carved with the words *"Keep your focus toward Heaven or chance a fall."*

Michael stepped toward the wall. "I wonder if this is the key we are looking for to decode the sequence of numbers in the last clue." He looked around. "I don't see a safe place to have hidden the ledger, but if Isabella hid it somewhere else, she may have used the message on the wall as part of her coded message to the ledger's location."

"Does it work as a key?"

He shrugged. "Let's find out." He took out a piece of paper that held the message they'd been working to decode. "The first two numbers in the sequence are one and four. If we assume first word, fourth letter, and the message on the wall represents the key in a usual left-to-right pattern, that means the clue would represent P. The first word is Keep and the fourth letter of the first word is P."

Harper paused. "We are going to need to write this down. Unfortunately, we didn't bring anything to write with."

"Maybe we can use a stick to write it in the mud on the ground."

"Good idea." She left the enclosed area and walked to the shrubs that had grown up all around the ruins. After finding a stick, she returned to where Michael was waiting. She located a spot on the ground that was muddy but not too wet and used the stick to write the first letter. "Okay, we have P; what's next?"

"A nine followed by a three, and then a five followed by a three."

"The clue would be the ninth word, third letter, which is L, followed by the fifth word, third letter, which is A. That would give us PLA."

"Next comes a seven followed by a one."

"Seventh word, first letter, is C. That gives us PLAC. What's next?"

"A one, followed by a two, and then a two, followed by another two."

"First word, second letter, is E and second word, second letter, is O, so that gives us PLACEO. What's next?"

"Three, one, two, four."

"F and R, which gives us PLACEOFR. And after that?"

"A five, followed by a two, and then a three, followed by a five, and then another four, followed by a one. That would be EST.

She stood up. "PLACEOFREST. Place of rest." She looked at Michael. "What was the rest of the clue?"

Michael looked down at the paper in his hand. "'Where angels sing their heavenly chorus for all eternity.'"

"Which gives us: Place of rest where angels sing their heavenly chorus for all eternity."

"The cemetery," they said in unison.

Harper clapped her hands together. "Of course. Manuel in the church said that the man who brought the stained-glass windows here and the woman he married are buried together in a cemetery not far from the church where the windows are now. That has to be where Isabella hid the ledger."

Michael reached out and hugged her. "Let's go."

******

The cemetery was deserted, which worked out fine as far as they were concerned. It was an old one, with headstones dating back more than a century.

"Manuel said that the man and woman were buried in the cemetery. If Isabella was a romantic who believed in true love despite her circumstances, I would imagine that she would have hidden the ledger near their graves."

Michael took her hand in his as they walked up and down each row, looking at the names of each husband, wife, child, sibling, and relative who had been buried there.

"I find cemeteries sad," she said.

"Why? Death is part of the circle of life."

"True. But some lives are long and rich with love and laughter, while others are brief and filled with pain and suffering." She paused. "I think my time overseas has caused me to look at life and its value somewhat differently. I have seen the underbelly of humanity. I have witnessed cruelty and suffering beyond description, and at some point, I suppose I'd seen enough death that I became numb to it. It's easier to look at the people who die at your hand as nonhumans who presented an obstacle to you carrying out your orders and were dealt with." She glanced at him. "But I have also seen humanity at its best. I have seen people give up their own lives so that total strangers might live. I have seen people rise to the challenge presented to them with courage and honor. I've witnessed the love that humans can show to one another when faced with impossible challenges in their daily lives."

Michael tightened his hand over hers but didn't respond. That, she decided, was actually the perfect response. A quiet acknowledgment of her experience without having the need to analyze it or offer advice.

Michael stopped at a grave. "Theodore Madison."

"And Anastasia Madison," she added. She swiped at a tear in the corner of her eye. "I hope they were as happy as Manuel seemed to think."

"It appears they were together until they were both very old," he pointed out. "I hope they were happy too."

Harper looked around. "Okay. I'm Isabella. I have a ledger that I hope to use to secure freedom and protection for both my baby and myself. There are men after me. I know I don't have long and it would be best to leave the ledger behind, so I hide it. Where?"

Michael stood next to her, scanning the area. "If it were an actual book of some sort, she would have looked for a place that was protected from the elements."

"And she would have looked for a place where visitors wouldn't stumble across it accidentally."

"I'd take a stab and guess she dug up either Theodore or Anastasia's grave and left the ledger with their remains, but a freshly dug grave would be too obvious."

Harper looked at the other graves closest to Theodore and Anastasia's. Thomas Madison lived to the ripe old age of seventy-two, but Helena Madison Lincoln died when she was only thirty-one; Steven Madison died when he was well into his sixties, while Angelica Madison died after only three days. "It looks like Theodore and Anastasia lost a baby girl. I would think that if Isabella was pregnant, that might strike a chord with her. The headstone is smaller than the others. It looks as if you could move it if you tried."

Michael pushed the headstone. Beneath it was something wrapped in a hand-knit shawl. He lifted it and returned the headstone to its resting place. He slowly unwrapped the garment to find a black leather book. "I think we found the ledger."

Chapter 19

It had been almost a week since Harper had said goodbye to Michael. Once they'd found the ledger, things happened quickly. They immediately headed north while Harper called Ben. He, in turn, called his FBI contact, Griswold, who agreed to meet them in Albuquerque. Given the fact that they were driving and he'd flown, he arrived not long after they did. After Michael used his hacking skills to delete every mention of Isabella's pregnancy or the existence of the baby from the thumb drive, they turned it and the ledger over to the agent, who thanked them and promised to keep them informed of any developments. As had been the plan, Michael and Harper drove to Minneapolis, where he caught a flight east for his parents' party and she drove the SUV Ben had provided to Moosehead. While she was thrilled to finally be reunited with Princess and

Bosley, and she was happy to see her family, there was a hole in her heart she knew could only be filled by a handsome computer geek with a lopsided grin and a heart the size of Texas.

"Five more minutes," she said to the puppy, who must have noticed her stirring in bed and decided it was time to play.

Bosley responded by pouncing on her head and biting at her hair.

So much for sleeping in.

Sliding her legs to the side, she sat on the side of the bed. Picking up the puppy, she cuddled him to her chest. It had been a difficult week as she'd tried to get her bearings after so many years away. She'd been a teenager when she'd left, not much more than a child, and now she was... actually, she didn't know what she was. She no longer felt like a child, but waking each morning in the room of her youth didn't allow her to feel much like an adult either.

Slipping her feet into her slippers, she pulled on a robe and walked toward the window. She'd always loved the view from the second story of the old farmhouse. The orchards in the distance were dormant now, but she knew come spring the trees would be covered in flowers that would give way to the sweet fruit produced by the trees Denver and Dixie had planted all those years ago. To the right of the orchard stood the old red barn. Haley had converted the old building into her own private living space, but when Harper had lived here as a child, the barn had been filled with horses, cows, and chickens.

After her dad died, her mother had decided that she was too busy building her veterinary practice to tend to so many animals, so the Hathaway family menagerie had been whittled down to six dogs, four cats, and an ornery old mule who would probably outlive them all.

"Should we go down to see if Dixie made breakfast?"

Bosley jumped around in a circle, as if communicating that breakfast sounded like a wonderful idea.

Harper picked up a brush from her dresser and ran it through her long dark hair. As a teen, she'd spent many an hour standing in front of this dresser with the attached mirror, dreaming of a future she could never quite define. Of all the Hathaway sisters, she had probably been the most unsettled. Hayden, the most ambitious and adventurous of the five, had always known she wanted to be a famous news reporter traveling the world after the next big story. Haley, the sister who most took after their father, had vowed at an early age to follow in Jagger's footsteps and become a carpenter. Harlow loved mysteries and baking. She'd often talked of being a writer, but owning a bookstore seemed to work for her. And Haven, the youngest of the girls, and the sibling who seemed to most mirror Dixie, was a free spirit who loved animals, music, art, and nature. She hadn't settled down quite yet, but she was young, and working as her mother's assistant when she wasn't traveling with her band seemed to work for her, at least for the time being.

She looked down at the puppy, who was staring at her with a look of confusion on his face. "You and I need to come up with a plan. As nice as it has been to be home, we can't lounge around forever."

The pup wagged his tail.

She opened the bedroom door and he shot down the stairs.

"Morning, darling. Oatmeal?" Dixie asked.

"Just coffee." Harper opened the back door for the puppy so that he could join the other dogs in the yard. Once she made sure the gate was closed, she shut the door, crossed the room, and sat down on a barstool opposite the woman with the long white braid draped over her bright yellow peasant top. "Did Mom go to work?"

"She did. Today is discount spay-and-neuter day, so I imagine she'll be busy lopping off danglies all day."

Harper grinned. "Yes, I imagine she will."

"I doubt we'll see her before dark. This is my poker day, so unless you go out for a bite, you'll be on your own for lunch."

"I think I can manage." She took a sip of the hot coffee. "Bosley and I plan to head over to Holly's. He misses playing with her dogs and she keeps telling me to come by as often as I'd like, so I suppose I will."

Dixie's pale blue eyes twinkled. "She still have that new baby?"

Harper nodded. It had been hard for her to keep the secret of who Bella was from her own family, but she'd decided it was something she needed to do to ensure the baby's safety until her father was no longer a threat.

Dixie poured what looked to be a quarter cup of sugar into her coffee. "She sure is a cute little thing. It's too bad that she is without her mother at such a young age."

Harper felt her heart constrict. "Yes. I feel for her. But Holly is great. In fact, I'd say that Ben and Holly represent the perfect parents. I don't think the baby is missing out on much."

Dixie passed a plate with homemade scones across the counter. Harper decided that a bite or two wouldn't hurt. Dixie was the best cook in the county. She'd missed many things about Moosehead, and her grandmother's cooking had neared the top of the list.

Dixie offered her homemade boysenberry jam for her scone. "So, are you ever going to get around to telling me the story of how you are connected to that baby?"

Harper raised a brow. "What makes you think I am connected to her at all?"

Dixie leaned forward on her elbows. "I may be getting on in years, but I promise you I still have all my faculties. It doesn't take a genius to see that you coming home in a car that belongs to Ben without a single item from your life in California, combined with a new puppy in the family that until you arrived had been living with Ben and Holly, and a new baby in the Holiday household who you have spent time with every single day since you've been back, adds up to a story waiting to be told."

Harper hesitated. "There is a story. But I'm afraid it is one that I've sworn not to tell."

Dixie nodded. "Fair enough. Are you in any sort of danger?"

"Not now."

"Okay, then. If you are going out today, would you mind stopping by the bookstore? Some of Harlow's mail ended up mixed in with ours again. I was going to drop it off on my way to poker, but Sylvia called to ask for a ride, so it would be out of my way to make the stop."

Harper nodded, relieved that Dixie had moved on from asking questions about Bella. "I'd be happy to. I've been wanting to stop by to take a look around. I can't believe that my little sister owns The Book Nook. I practically lived in that place when I was a kid."

"You won't recognize it. Harlow's done a lot to fix the place up."

"A renovation was probably called for. I loved hanging out at The Book Nook, but I do remember it being dark and dusty. Most of the time, the books were just set out in boxes that you had to dig through to find what you wanted."

"Harlow has totally changed the feel of the place. She painted all those dark bookshelves white and stripped that old wallpaper and painted the walls a light blue. The old carpet is gone and the hardwood floors beneath were refinished. She even set up a lounge where the old storeroom used to be. She sells baked goods and offers coffee and tea there. There are tables and chairs and even sofas where you can while away a winter's day and read."

"It sounds charming. I'll stop by after I visit with Holly. Maybe I'll grab lunch for Harlow and me from the deli next door."

"Can't. It closed down a decade ago. There is a pizza place a few doors down that is pretty good, though, and of course there is always Dolly's Place."

Harper smiled at the memory of the restaurant where she'd enjoyed many a burger during her high school years. "Is Dolly still running the place?"

"For now. She has it up for sale, though."

"Oh, that's too bad. Why is she selling?"

"Her daughter moved to Florida and she decided to move there with her. Makes sense from a lot of different angles. I think the cold is bothering her more and more the older she gets, and she has three adorable grandbabies that she rarely gets to see now."

Harper took a sip of her coffee. "It does sound like moving might be the best decision. I'll miss her burgers, but everyone deserves an opportunity to reinvent themselves." Harper looked across the counter at the seventy-five-year-old woman who never seemed to age. "Do you ever get the urge to leave Moosehead and do other things? Reinvent yourself?"

Dixie chuckled. "Lordy Bee, no. I've lived on this land almost my entire life and I plan to be buried here. Or at least to have my ashes spread out in the orchard next to Denver's. Denver and I have been a team for a good long time. I spent my life with him, and I plan to spend eternity with him as well."

"I get that. This is your home. I guess it wouldn't make sense to move at this stage in your life."

"If by 'this stage' in my life you mean my prime, I agree. I love Moosehead and this farm. Besides, it took me seventy-five years to perfect the package you see before you today. Why on earth would I want to start again?"

Harper smiled, leaned forward, and hugged her grandmother. "I can't think of a single thing you'd want to change."

Dixie ran a thumb over her cheek. "It's good to have you home, baby girl."

"It's good to be home."

******

Like the Hathaway farm, the Holiday farm featured a huge old farmhouse, a rustic barn, and acres and acres of land that stretched as far as the eye could see. And like the Hathaway farmhouse, Holly's home was decorated for the upcoming holiday with natural garland and homemade decorations. Holly had first come to Moosehead as a baby without an identity. After graduating high school, she'd moved to New York and started her own advice column, which was widely popular and currently syndicated and published in newspapers and magazines across the country. After Holly inherited the farmhouse that had been run as a foster home during her childhood, she'd decided to move her base of operation to Moosehead and continue the legacy her own foster mother had left her.

"I have news," Holly said after hugging Harper hello and escorting Bosley through the eclectic farmhouse and out into the yard to the other dogs.

"Good news, I hope." Harper crossed the room and picked up the baby, who had been sleeping in her infant carrier. God, she had missed her. The highlight of her days since returning to Moosehead had been coming by for a cuddle.

"The best news. Ben and his FBI buddy worked it out for Bella to get a new identity. She will get a new birth certificate and a history that does not involve either Isabella Fernandez or Salvador Garcia in any way. No one will ever know who she was or how she started out."

Harper grinned as the baby pursed her lips. "That's wonderful. Are you sure there won't be a paper trail of any sort back to Isabella?"

"Ben says no. He says that all links to her past will be permanently dissolved."

Harper let out a breath of relief. "That's great. I know the only thing that really mattered to Isabella was that her daughter was safe and that she was offered the opportunity for a normal life." Harper frowned. "I guess that means she will be put up for adoption."

Holly offered Harper a sincere look. "Not necessarily. Bella is not in the system. No one knows she's here. Ben said he can work it out for us to keep her if we decide we want to do that, and the paper trail will support the idea that we were the ones to adopt her. Having said that, it would be just as easy to fix the paperwork to show that you are her adoptive mother. Ben and I both want to give you the chance to raise her if you want to."

Harper felt a catch in her chest. "As much as I want to, I can't. It wouldn't be fair to her. Not only am I single but I don't have a job, a future, or even a permanent place to live. My life is too unsettled to bring a baby into it."

Holly took Harper's hand in hers. "While I would never encourage anyone who didn't feel ready for a baby to adopt one, I'd hate to see you make a decision you'll regret later. Fate seems to have brought you and Bella together. Yes, I do agree that the timing could be better because your life does seem a bit unsettled. But you aren't alone. You have a big extended family of people who love you, and I'm sure Dixie and your mom would welcome both you and the baby into their home. You may not have a job right now, but you are a brave, strong, intelligent woman. I'm sure there are tons of opportunities out there just waiting to be found. You may not be married, but single women raise children all the time. Besides, you have Michael, and I suspect he would make an excellent uncle if nothing else. And you have Ben and me, who, of course, would be willing to babysit and help out in any other way you needed."

Harper hesitated.

Holly's deep blue eyes grew serious. "If you decide not to adopt her, Ben will arrange for the adoption paperwork to bear our name. You have a few days to decide if you want to think about it."

Harper let out a long breath. "I do love Bella, and I want what is best for her. I'm not sure what's best for her is me, but I'll think about it."

"Please do," Holly said as Ben walked in the front door with two brown-haired preschoolers.

"Bosley is here," one of the twins shouted as he ran toward the back door.

"It's my turn to play with him first," his identical twin shouted as he ran after him.

Ben chuckled. "The boys sure love that puppy. I think we may need to consider an addition to the family."

"We already have six dogs," Holly countered.

"But none of them are puppies," Ben pointed out. "Jake Fitzpatrick has lab puppies. I stopped by to look at them today. There is one that looks a lot like Bosley. Just imagine the look on their faces when they see that Santa brought them a brand new puppy."

Holly groaned and rolled her eyes, but even Harper could see that Joe and Reggie Holiday had a new puppy in their future. She'd considered leaving

Bosley with them, but her mom didn't mind him being at the farm, and the energetic puppy seemed to fill at least part of the hole in her heart left by Bella and Michael.

"Holly was filling me in on the good news," Harper said to Ben.

"I have additional news that I am anxious to share, so I am glad you are here."

"I hope it's good."

Ben nodded. "The ledger you and Michael found contained not only dates and locations of past meets but future ones as well. The DEA was able to use the information to stake out one that had been mentioned between Garcia and one of his major distributors at the Port of Los Angeles. Long story short, Garcia died during the arrest and his distributor is in custody."

Harper nodded. "I am so relieved. What about Loughlin, the CHP officer who shot Agent Beaverton?"

"Also dead. And the DEA mole is dead as well. We suspect that Garcia did a bit of housekeeping before the attempted capture. I can't say for certain that there aren't any other bad guys out there, but I do think that with Garcia's death, no one is going to be looking for either you or Bella, and even if someone knew about the baby, there is not a single link between Bella and the child Isabella gave birth to."

Harper sighed in relief. It looked like the chase was finally over. Now all she needed to do was to find a way to get over Michael, who hadn't called once in the week since he left, and figure out what to do about Bella, a baby she very much wanted but wondered if she could care for.

Chapter 20

Michael stood on his parents' front porch and looked out toward the sea as he waited for the cab that would take him to the airport. He hadn't wanted to come home, but now he was glad he had. There was something about the tide rolling toward the snowy shore that seemed to calm his soul. Sure, it had stung more than just a bit to see his twin brother with the woman he had once wanted to spend his life with, but after meeting Harper, he had realized that what he felt for Julia was pale in comparison to what he felt for a woman he had only known a couple of weeks. Perhaps Matthew had done him a favor when he'd prevented him from marrying someone he'd only thought he loved.

"I thought I'd find you out here hiding," Megan said as she stepped out onto the porch from the house.

"I just needed some air so I decided to wait out here for my cab. It's a great party, Meg. Mom and Dad are lucky to have at least one child who makes sure that things like anniversaries are celebrated."

Meg walked over to Michael and rested her head on his shoulder. "I think it is important that we remember that we are a family. I know things sort of fell apart when Maddie died, and it was a long time before we felt like celebrating anything, but if she had been old enough to understand such things, I suspect that she wouldn't have wanted her death to act as a catalyst for the death of the whole family." Meg took a deep breath. "If it had been me who died, I know I wouldn't want my legacy to be one of destruction and despair."

Michael put his arm around his sister's shoulders. "I know. And I think Mom and Dad have finally figured that out too. They seemed genuinely happy today. And it was time for me to mend fences with Matthew and Julia. I'm grateful you badgered me into coming."

Meg raised a brow, tipping her face toward his. "You are?"

He nodded. "I am. I know you wanted me to stay for Christmas and I might have but I have something important to take care of but maybe we can do a big family Christmas next year. I think I've actually decided to move to Moosehead. My plan is to buy a house large enough for the entire family to visit."

Meg let out a long breath. "Really? I have to admit that I'm surprised that you've decided to make the move but a house large enough for the entire family to spend the holidays together would be awesome. Of course, convincing Macy and Marley to show up will be the real challenge."

"We have a year to convince them."

Meg smiled. "It would be great to get the entire family together. You know I'm in but it's going to be harder to convince Macy to come home. She took Maddie's death harder than any of us. She was the oldest. She'd been put in charge. I know she blames herself for Maddie's death every day of her life."

Michael sighed. "Yeah. She has said as much to me. And I understand. It did seem as if Mom and Dad blamed her at first."

Michael and Matthew had gone off fishing and their parents had been invited sailing, so Macy was put in charge of her three younger sisters. She was on the phone with her boyfriend and hadn't even realized that Maddie had wandered into the water until it was too late. In a way, the family had lost both of them that day. Maddie drowned and Macy drifted away. She lived in Alaska now, and Michael hadn't seen her in years.

"Have you heard when Marley might be back from her romp around Europe?" Michael asked.

Megan shrugged. "She hasn't said, but the last time I spoke to her it seemed like she was getting restless. I'd be willing to bet she will be home by summer. Of course, I have no idea where I'll be."

"Job hunt still giving you fits?"

Megan nodded. "I just lost a job to a guy who probably didn't do as well in medical school as I did, but he did a stint with Doctors Without Borders, and, from what I've heard, diversity in a résumé holds a lot more water than I expected."

"So all your experience at a top-rated hospital is actually hurting your chance of getting a job at those same hospitals?"

Meg nodded. "Ironic, isn't it?"

"Maybe you need to spice up your résumé. Do some work in a rural setting."

Meg turned to look her brother in the eye. "Macy said much the same thing when we were chatting in one of our weekly FaceTime sessions."

"You FaceTime with Macy every week?"

Meg glanced at him. "She is my sister."

"I know, but she is my sister too and I haven't spoken to her in years. I guess I'm just surprised to hear you had stayed in touch."

Megan shrugged. "I keep up with everyone. It is my job as the middle sister. So, back to my problem."

Michael turned slightly. "I think a gig in a rural setting is a good idea. Not only because I agree that it would provide diversity to your résumé but because I think you could use some time to focus on you. You spend a lot of time taking care of everyone else and making sure that everyone is happy, but I think you need to take time to make sure that you are happy."

"I'm happy."

"Are you?"

Meg glanced away, but Michael could see a tear in her eye. "Are you sure you can't stay a few more days?" She asked. "I know you have a cab coming but if you want to send it away I can take you to the airport in a few days."

"I really do need to get back. I actually have some showings for homes in Moosehead set up for tomorrow.'

"Tomorrow? Why the rush?" Her eyes widened. "There's a woman behind this sudden urge to move." She paused and continued. "The woman you just drove halfway across the country with. I should have realized."

Michael hesitated. He knew he was ready to commit to Harper and Bella but Harper had only recently lost her fiancé and he'd vowed to give her the time he was sure she would need to get over his death. Still, in the week since he'd seen her he felt like he was going crazy. He couldn't eat, he couldn't sleep; he was a total mess, which was where the idea of making the move to Moosehead came in. Maybe Harper wasn't ready for a relationship quite yet, but he hoped she was ready for a friend who would be there every step of the way as she worked to rebuild her life and create a new life for Bella. "I will admit that meeting Harper gave me the push I needed to actually call my realtor, but you know I've been considering the move for a while now."

She lifted a brow. He could see that she was about to say more but his cab pulled up sparing him the inquisition.

He reached out and hugged his sister. "It looks like my ride is here. Thanks again for everything. I'll invite you out for a stay as soon as I get settled."

"I hope so. I can't wait to meet your girl."

"She's not my girl. "

Meg just laughed and waved as he climbed into the cab and sped away.

Chapter 21

Harper glanced in her rearview mirror at the baby sleeping in her car seat. It had only been a few days since she'd brought Bella home to the farmhouse where she'd grown up after deciding to adopt her, but somehow, she felt different. She supposed that being completely responsible for another person was something she would have to get used to. The thought of the task she had taken on both terrified and fulfilled her. Every time she held Bella in her arms, she experienced a kind of love she had never known, yet when the baby looked at her with such trust in her eyes, she was terrified that she wouldn't measure up.

She wasn't alone in this, and that thought gave her comfort. Her grandmother, her mom, and her sisters were all great. Haley had been helping her turn the spare bedroom into a nursery with an adjoining door to her own room, and the mural Haven had been busily painting on the wall was so incredibly perfect that it made her want to cry every time she looked at it. Glancing at the puppy on the seat beside her, she realized that she had everything she needed. Well, almost. She still hadn't heard from Michael, and that both hurt and frightened her. Had she misread the feelings she thought they had both begun to develop? Had his trip home only renewed his love for Julia? Had he realized that what they had never could or would compare?

She slowed as she approached the address Ben had given her. He'd asked her to drive out to the lake to pick up Bella's new birth certificate, which she'd been happy to do. She knew he kept a house at the lake that also doubled as his office, but the house attached to the address he'd given her was huge. All this time, she'd been picturing something smaller.

Parking in front of the house, she opened the door and let Bosley out. She went around to the side of the car and opened the back door. Being careful not to wake her, she gently lifted the baby into her arms. Slinging the diaper bag over her shoulder, she headed up the walkway that, fortunately, someone had shoveled.

There was a note on the door, telling her to come right in. She opened the heavy wood door and stepped into the tile entry, which opened up to a great room with a wall of windows that looked out over the lake. Cradling the baby to her chest, she slipped off her wet shoes before stepping onto the wood flooring of the living area. The floor-to-ceiling, river-rock fireplace that rose two stories into the air dominated the wall to the right of the windows where an open dining and kitchen area had been strategically placed to the left.

"Wow." Was this the cabin Ben kept for a retreat and office? The place had to be five or six thousand square feet at least.

Turning when she heard a sound behind her, she gasped. "Michael! What are you doing here?"

He bent down to greet Bosley, who was jumping on him, demanding that he acknowledge his existence. "I live here. Or at least I will, once the escrow is complete and I have a chance to move."

"Live here?" She stepped back and looked at the huge, two-story house. "In this ginormous house?"

"Do you like it?"

"I love it, but I thought you said you lived in Minneapolis."

"I do. I mean I did." Michael took a deep breath and blew it out slowly. "Perhaps I should start again."

Harper just looked at him.

"I've missed you."

Harper smiled. "I've missed you too."

"I tried to take a step back and give you the time you needed, but after a miserable couple of weeks without you, I realized I was never going to survive being the noble gentleman I truly wanted to be, so I put in an offer on this house. I figured that living here at the lake would give me the opportunity to be part of your life, as well as the lives of Bella and Bosley, while still giving you the time and space you need."

Harper frowned. "The time and space I need? Who said I needed time and space?"

It was Michael's turn to frown. "Don't you? I just figured…"

Harper took a step forward, cradling the baby between their bodies. She leaned forward and touched Michael's lips gently with her own. "You figured wrong."

Chapter 22
The Following Year

"I can't feel my feet," Harper said, as she followed Michael through knee deep snow in search of the perfect Christmas tree. While December days in northern Minnesota were traditionally chilly, today's temperature was downright arctic.

"I will admit that when I came up with the idea while you and I and Bella were watching that movie last week it hadn't occurred to me how cold it would actually be."

Harper glanced at the baby in the pack on Michael's back. She was bundled from head to toe and appeared to be warm and happy. Not only was Bella giggling at the antics of the now fully grown lab in the deep snow, but Bosley seemed to be having a wonderful time in spite of the chill as well. "Your idea was a good one and Bella and Bosley both seem to be having the time of their lives but for the sake of my toes I'm going to suggest we just grab that tall tree we saw when we first parked. It's close to the road, and it's tall enough to fill the entry. I will admit that the backside is pretty bare but we'll just put that side against the wall."

"And the tree for the main living area?"

"There is a gorgeous twenty-footer displayed at the back of the lot in town," Harper reminded him.

Michael hesitated but then smiled. "The tree in the lot in town will be fine for the living area as will the tree closest to the road for the entry. I guess it is a lot colder than I anticipated it would be, but I really wanted our first Christmas together as a family to be a memorable one."

"And it has been," Harper agreed, jumping up and down in an attempt to stay warm. "The long shopping weekend to the city to pick up gifts for our huge extended families was magical, and you know how Bella loved the Santa's Village in town. I thought she might cry when we sat her on Santa's lap but she just smiled and pulled on his beard."

Michael smiled. "Our girl is the fearless sort. Just like her mama." He turned and started back down the mountain. Harper followed. "Maybe I'll call the lot in town and just have the tree we already have our eye on delivered. That way we can grab the tree for the entry and then head home to warm up."

"Warming up sounds perfect," Harper agreed. "And there is a Christmas Movie on tonight that I wanted to watch."

"Hallmark?"

"Die Hard."

He smiled. "Ah. Of course. I should have known." He glanced over his shoulder at the toddler in the pack on his back. "You know that by next Christmas Bella will be old enough to watch TV with us. At least some of the time. We'll need to trade Die Hard for Frosty the Snowman or Rudolph the Red Nosed Reindeer."

"I like Rudolph. When I was little I was completely fascinated by the idea of Santa's Village and wanted to visit more than anything, but now that I'm older and realize that Santa lives way up there in the North Pole, which is even colder than here, I'm less enchanted with the idea."

"You grew up in Minnesota I would think you'd be used to the cold."

"I spent years and years in tropical locations chasing the next dive. I keep thinking my tolerance for the cold will come back but so far that hasn't happened. By the way, speaking of cold, is Marley still planning to come for Christmas?"

Michael nodded. "Marley and Meg will both be here, as will my parents, my brother Matthew, and Julia."

"Still no word from Macy?"

He frowned. "No. And I have to admit that I'm getting a little worried about that."

"She hasn't contacted anyone in the family?"

215

"Not since she called my parents in October asking about a loan to get her plane fixed. At the time she told my dad that she had a series of charters booked to locations not served by internet or cell service so she might be off grid for a while, and this isn't the first time Macy has fallen off the face of the earth for an extended period of time, but I will admit that this time feels different."

"Do you think she is in some sort of trouble?"

He frowned. "I don't know. I hope not." He stopped walking as he approached a tree. "Is this the one you were talking about?"

"It is," Harper confirmed. "I'll get Bella strapped into the truck while you chop it down. Maybe, just maybe, if we get the heater going right away I'll come away from this experience with all my fingers and toes."

She stood on tip toe and kissed Bella on the cheek before unbuckling her from her pack. As she transferred her to the truck she thought over the past year. Last December had gotten off to a rocky start with the death of Bella's biological mother and the cross-country road trip to find the answers needed to keep Bella safe, but this holiday season had been magical and enchanting and without a doubt the best of her life. She'd never been the sort to enjoy shopping for shopping's sake but this year, with Bella to buy gifts for, she'd gone just a little shopping crazy. Harper never wanted children of her own, at least she hadn't thought she did, but she knew Michael wanted Bella to have brothers and sisters, and her memories of a loud and crowded house no longer generated the same negative feelings they once had, so maybe, just maybe, by this time next year she and Michael would have two little darlings to shop for.

USA Today best-selling author Kathi Daley lives in beautiful Lake Tahoe with her husband Ken. When she isn't writing, she likes spending time hiking the miles of desolate trails surrounding her home. Find out more about her books at www.kathidaley.com

Made in the USA
Middletown, DE
27 September 2023